Cover Design and Interior Format

Trusting a
SCOT

THE SOULMATE CHRONICLES ~ TWO

KEIRA
MONTCLAIR

AUTHOR'S NOTE

As you will often see in historical fiction, authors use artistic license to change some facts to fit their needs. While some of the events in this story are based on true events, the timeline has been adjusted to fit my story.

PROLOGUE

Heaven

GRAEME BREATHED IN THE SALTINESS of the sea air, a bright smile crossing his face. How he loved the beach. This was his favorite spot in the entire world.

But he was missing something...or rather someone.

Where was Catherine? Although they'd been reunited after the last lifetime they'd spent together on Earth, they'd parted, briefly, to visit others in their family. Both of them knew it was the last chance they'd get for some time. Their next challenge was nearly upon them. They'd agreed to meet as soon as they felt the summons. She'd told him she would come to him. Here, it required only a thought.

Yet the time had come—he felt the strange tugging sensation—and Catherine had not yet arrived.

Finally, he saw her. Off in the distance, a beautiful young woman ran across the water toward him, laughing as the ebbing flow of the tide teased her feet. Her hair danced over her shoulders in long, red waves, moving with the rhythm of the wind. He stood still, drinking in his soulmate's beauty, her carefree attitude, and her laughter.

When she was nearly upon him, he opened his arms and she flew into them. He hugged her, then kissed her deeply. "I've missed you."

"And I've missed you. It's hard to believe it's already time for a new mission. Another life."

He glanced over her shoulder, surprised to see someone he didn't recognize heading toward them from the rocky expanse behind the beach. He'd expected Evangeline, the angel they'd worked with in the past. She waved and hurried to their side. "Hello. Evangeline won't be with you this time, but I'm here as your guiding angel. My name is Tessa." Her features were striking, from her long brown hair to her deep hazel eyes, and she gave off an aura of peace and tranquility. She *felt* like an angel. The colorful skirt and teal top she wore fit their tropical setting.

"Greetings to you, Tessa. So nice to meet you," Catherine shouted, hoping to be heard over the din of the ocean waves. "It's a lovely area. Did you choose this?"

"No, this was Graeme's choice...or his heaven, I'd call it. Just like your version of heaven is decorated with jewels. I heard all about it from Evangeline."

"Yes," he said, giving her another quick kiss. "Just you and me, the sand, the sun, and the heat."

"Lovely," she whispered so only he could hear

her words. "And so right for us."

"Where to next? I'm assuming that's the reason why you're here." Graeme moved Catherine to his side, then led her to a shady spot amidst some trees. "It's easier to speak here." Tessa joined them. Three chairs appeared miraculously, along with a platter of fresh fruit and tall glasses of iced tea.

"In your quest to achieve guiding angelship, you are aware you must travel to Earth and live amongst humans. Your own guardian angels will be there to help you find each other, and once you come together, you must stay together. Your goal is to help foster peace among the people around you, end as much human suffering as possible, and, of course, do good wherever you go. This is your second test. You'll be born in your new lives tomorrow, so enjoy the sun and the sand!"

Tessa turned to leave, but Catherine stopped her. "A few questions, please?"

She smiled and nodded to her, holding her hand out to indicate she would accept her questions.

"We won't recognize each other as soulmates?"

"No, it will be the same as before. You'll have an instinctive reaction to each other. Something will catch your attention when you first meet, but you won't understand why. Your charms will also draw you to each other—your necklace, Catherine, and Graeme's stone from his father."

"And will we have the same names?"

"You may, but probably not."

"What happens if we don't listen to our guiding angels?" Graeme asked. "Or the charms?"

"You'll be given several opportunities through-out your lives to meet up. Most soulmates do take advantage of the second or third times their paths cross."

"Anything else?"

"Where are we going this time?"

"Back to Scotland. Good luck to both of you."

CHAPTER ONE

Spring, 1297, Lowlands of Scotland

CARA BRECKENRIDGE SWUNG HER DAGGER out in front of her, aiming for her husband's belly as hard and fast as she could, but he grabbed her hand and spun her around in a second.

He held her blunted dagger to her throat and said, "Mayhap ye are no' capable of learning. What will it take for ye to listen to me and do as I tell ye? Ye're no different at fighting than ye are at anything else." His long blond hair fell across his eyes, blocking his vision.

Cara stomped down on his foot, crunching the boot of her heel down as hard as she could. He let go of her with a yelp.

"Why did ye do that? This is practice!" he bellowed. Their two young lads, watching off to the side, moved to hide behind a tree.

"Brice, Bryan, 'tis all right. Ye need no' hide from yer father." George wiped his brow as he stared at her. "Cara, I'm trying to teach ye. Ye have no call to get nasty." He stood with his hands on his hips, his breathing coming faster than she'd expected. It would have made her prouder if she weren't gasping for air. She hated that sparring took her so much more effort than it did him.

"I'm trying my best. Ye tell me to fight ye off. If I cannae do it with my dagger, I'll use my feet."

He shook his head and bent over at the waist. "'Tis enough for today. 'Struth, I know no' if I can ever teach ye. We've tried for a fortnight and ye're no better than when we started. Go inside and get supper for the lads and me." He waved her toward the door of their small hut, dismissing her.

As she headed back inside, she tucked the dagger into the pocket she'd sewn inside her gown. Her husband's dismissal hurt, but she didn't wish to show it. He never believed in her. While she knew he was a good man, always providing for her and the lads, he'd become cold and hard of late. Though he often apologized for his attitude, he never made any move to change it.

Scotland had fallen into hard times after the death of their king, Alexander III. King Edward had chosen a new king, John Balliol, but he was just a name holder. Edward did whatever he wished, and his wishes often crushed the will and spirit of the Scottish people, which had sparked them to attempt to choose a new king. William Wallace and Robert the Bruce both fought hard to show their qualifications for the job, among others.

King Edward's response was death and torture to all who stood in his way. He'd taken Berwick in the name of the English—a brutish attack that had left deep wounds—and was moving deeper into Scotland. All of the Scots felt uneasy. Bitter, even.

It was worse for those who resided in the Lowlands. Cara and her family lived in a small village outside the Breckenridge Castle, where George's brother, Cathill, lived and handled the tenants. They all paid him with part of their crop production for the right to stay outside his home, and this was done in return for protection.

Except Cathill had gathered his entire family and headed into the Highlands to stay with some cousins in a large clan. They'd taken most of the protection with them.

Cara had begged to go along, but George had insisted he'd stay and train the remaining men to fight. Cara and their lads, too. But word reached them every day of more villages that had been destroyed and burned, all the people killed.

Nightmares consumed Cara's sleep. She feared for their lads, but George refused to take them to safety. It was their land, he said, *Scottish* land, and he'd not forsake it.

He said the same thing every time they began practicing in the morn. "My brother can run away, but I'll not run like some bairn. Once we fight the English off, we'll move into Breckenridge Castle. Will Cathill not be surprised when he returns to find us living there?"

"Can we not go now?" she'd often ask. An imperfect solution, but at least the castle walls would offer some protection.

"Nay, the English always attack the castles. They may be lenient with small villages, but if they attack, we'll stand and protect what's ours. We've all trained hard and our work will be rewarded."

And yet, Cara could not help but doubt him. Part of her felt he cared more for his principles than he did his family. Something else drove him, too—his bitterness over what he perceived as his brother's desertion. He spat in the dirt whenever his brother's name was mentioned, just as he did when anyone spoke of the English.

Cara started cutting up vegetables to add to the stew bubbling over the hearth, and after a while, Bryan came in behind her with a pitcher of goat's milk. "Here, Mama. For dinner."

She thanked him and continued to work.

"Mama," Bryan whispered. The older of the two lads at eight, he'd become very protective of her and his brother. "I think ye did a fine job. Ye're verra strong."

Cara reached down and rustled his dark red hair. "Many thanks to ye. I just need to work harder. Papa is right. If the English come, we must be prepared."

"I've been practicing verra hard. I'll kill anyone who touches ye or Brice."

"I know ye will." She knew he wouldn't be able to, but she wasn't the type to disparage someone's efforts when they tried their best.

Unlike her husband. Of late, her meals were tasteless to him, her sewing not tight enough, and their lovemaking…well, she'd not think any more on it.

She just vowed to try harder on the morrow.

✎

Gabriel Montgomerie was a wanderer.

He had been unmoored by his wife's death, by the tragedy that would haunt him forever.

Something else haunted him: the face of the bastard who'd been responsible for Della's death.

He'd heard all his acquaintances' kind words, but no pretty sentiment could bring back his dear sweet wife, the one woman whose smile could light up his heart. Nor could they avenge her death. Their pity had somehow made it all worse.

The thirst for revenge had consumed him.

And so he had left the area he'd been born in and the people who knew him best. Gabriel's father was English, and although he'd died a few years back, his travels had brought him to his family. They'd informed him that the English were searching for an able-bodied man to lead various charges into Scotland. The ability to speak Gaelic was particularly prized since few of the English could understand Highlanders.

Except Gabriel could. He'd decided to keep his talent to himself, however, so he could use it to eavesdrop on important men.

After searching for placement with one of the groups, the perfect opportunity had presented itself. He'd accepted the job of marshal for Thorley Tremaine, Baron of Hepple, one of the king's favored barons. The baron had been desperate for a new marshal, for his man had disappeared just before they were to cross the border. Or so he said. The rumors Gabriel had heard were more disturbing, but Gabriel had seen his opportunity and jumped on it.

They'd been traveling for about a moon now, on the move ever since King Edward's victory in the Battle of Dunbar. The English had taken the castle in his name, and the Scots had finally accepted defeat, giving in to their king's demand. Late one night, the baron's company settled into a quiet meadow in the Lowlands. The moon was covered with clouds and the air was bitterly cold, but not so cold they couldn't survive outside.

Gabriel approached the baron around the fire, where they'd cooked the meat of a boar they'd killed on their voyage. The men had eaten heartily, knowing they were unlikely to eat this well again for many days.

One of the squires, Wyot Darcy, rocked back and forth on a log. Gabriel realized he hadn't seen him eat a bite. The lad was a fellow wanderer. Gabriel had met him in the Borderlands and taken a liking to him. He'd brought him into the baron's service, and though the boy was doing well, he was only five and ten and not immune to the atrocities of war. Some of the sights they'd encountered from the aftermath of various battles and skirmishes had sickened him. But it had been some time since they'd seen anything like that, and the lad was so thin he couldn't afford to lose more weight.

"Wyot, you should eat," he said. "We may not eat

this well for quite some time."

The boy stared up at him, clutching his belly. "Something is cramping my belly now, my lord. I do not wish to eat yet." Suddenly, his eyes widened and he jumped off the log and ran off to the copse of trees not far away.

"That'll make you feel better. Get it out so you can eat some fresh meat," Gabriel called out after him, chuckling to himself. He knew exactly how the lad felt. It wasn't easy getting used to eating on the road. You went with an empty belly more often than a full one, and sickness was never far away.

Dunstan Stoddard, Hepple's steward, grimaced. "He better get rid of it and not give it to the rest of us. Besides, we won't have much to eat for long. Our king said the supplies are running thin in the Lowlands. We didn't start with much, so we'll have to find what we can on the road. I doubt we'll get lucky with another boar anytime soon."

"We have thirty mouths to feed," Hepple said with a shrug. "We'll take food wherever we find it, and we'll kill any who try to stop us."

Since Wyot had left and the knights all sat around a different fire, Gabriel decided to ask the question that had been foremost in his mind. "And what of the women and children we meet along the way? We haven't seen any yet. Have you orders on how to handle them?" It hadn't happened yet, for which he was grateful, but he knew it would happen eventually. When it did, he prayed Hepple would leave them be.

Hepple cocked his head as if considering the

question. "We do as our king has ordered. We burn the villages and kill everyone whom we pass on our way to Bothwell Castle. Then we are to overtake it if any Scots have gone back in. That will be our primary headquarters and we will hold it in the name of King Edward. We'll go wherever we're needed from there. It's a simple plan. I only have one other order and that is to find a female spy. He wants a Scot we can threaten and intimidate. I am to send her to Edinburgh Castle so she can make her way into the graces of the Scots who have sworn fealty to him. He fears some are liars, and he's undoubtedly right. A woman will be the best to ferret out the traitors. To answer your question, we will kill all we meet but for one comely female."

He couldn't help himself. "That's a little cruel, don't you think?"

Hepple glared at him, and Stoddard stopped his chewing to see how the baron would respond. "I see it as an act of kindness. Without their men or their food stores, they'll all starve or freeze to death. If you don't view it the same way, I'll have to question your loyalty."

Gabriel bit his tongue and dug his fingers into his palm. They were every bit as cruel as they were reputed to be.

Murderers. He was traveling with a group of guiltless murderers.

CHAPTER TWO

CARA BENT AT THE WAIST and charged at her husband, then did her best to direct her blunted weapon upward at his belly, but she couldn't. Today, they had a few more observers. Their sons watched, but also some of the villagers.

"'Twas a bit better, Cara," he said, giving her a small nod of acknowledgement. "You would have slowed the man, without a doubt. I need to spend time training with the other villagers now. As you know, the enemy is drawing close."

News had arrived of approaching forces, and they all feared what was to come. Their chances of repelling the English were dimming with each passing day.

She smiled and thanked him, then moved inside to wash some of their clothing. Brice, her wee lad, followed her. "Mama, can we not go where our uncles went?" he asked in a small voice. "Why must we stay?"

"Oh, sweetling, we must stay with Papa," she said, gathering their clothes. "We'll fight together if we're attacked."

"But what if we're stolen away? I heard the other lads talk about kidnapping, about them stealing the boys to make them fight or take care of armor. They willnae take me from ye, will they?" She set the clothes on the table, and her son rested his chin in his hand on top of the wooden surface, his big green eyes searching hers for some guarantee they'd be safe.

"Nay, laddie." It was a pleasant lie. She couldn't bear to tell him the truth about the danger they faced, not when there was no protecting him from it. She ruffled his hair, which was the same exact color as her own. "And if anything like that ever happened, know that yer papa and I would travel to the end of England to find ye. We would never give up." She gave him a swift hug, squeezing him tight, and then tickled his belly. "I'd fight my way back to ye, I would."

His laughter was the sweetest music she could ever hear. When she went to the washstand, Brice tagged along behind her, grabbing her hand for support every once in a while. That told her the poor lad was truly frightened. And so was she. Would they survive an attack?

She wasn't given much time to think on it. An hour later, the sounds outside the hut changed. More rustling, shouting, and her husband's voice finally carried to her across the wind. "Cara, get yer dagger!"

Heart jumping into her throat, she ran to the door of the hut, looking down the path toward the rumbling of horses' hooves. Brice had gone outside to join his father and brother, and she heard him screaming for her. She ran outside to her boys and took hold of Brice's hand while Bryan stood next to his sire.

Down the path came a cavalry of horses, led by armored knights.

"Cara, ye must fight. Get your dagger and stand behind me!"

She looked up at her husband in shock. "George, the men are knights in armor. How can we hope to fight them?" Her gaze hung on the path, on the knights bearing down at them.

"Usually, there are only knights in the front line. The others will be men just like me. And they all have flesh, just like me. Even the knights in armor. There are places you can plunge your knife into. Ye must do it or we'll all die."

"Mayhap they are just passing through. Until we see what they are about, I wish to hide with the lads."

He whirled at her and said, "Dinnae hide. Ye'll fight as I taught ye."

Anger and bitterness hung on his every word, and she saw in his eyes that he meant to fight no matter what. Even if it was the death of all of them. The truth glared at her.

She'd not have any of it, instead vowing to do what she could to keep herself and her lads alive. Although she knew Bryan would never go against his father, no matter what she said or did, she could at least protect Brice. Their best chance was to hide before the knights moved past them.

Other children around them began to scream as the cloud of dust came toward them, hearkening in a massive number of horses unlike anything they'd ever seen.

Brice began to scream and clutched her skirts.

George grabbed her wrist, hard enough that it hurt, and said, "Ye'll stay and fight."

"Nay, I'm hiding. I cannae fight an armored man. How could I when I couldnae even fight you when ye had no armor? I'm no' a fool. I must protect our sons." She tried to yank her arm from him, but he wouldn't let her go.

"Ye'll fight next to me. If I go, we all go. Every one of us. Ye and Brice must fight!"

"George, have ye no' lost yer mind? How can Brice fight? He's only five and couldn't hurt any knight. Leave us be. I'll hide him as best I can and use my dagger if I must."

George pulled her up to his face, so close that his spittle hit her cheek when he spoke. "I'm ordering ye to stay and fight."

He gave her no choice. She kicked him hard and he dropped her hand in a reflex action, giving her just enough time to run off. Pulling her gaze from him, she picked Brice up and raced toward the forest, praying to find a good hiding place.

"Cara! If we die. 'twill be your fault!"

Now she knew her husband had gone daft. That was the most ridiculous statement she'd ever heard. Did he really think she could put an end to a line of knights holding swords and battleaxes with her wee dagger?

She ran as fast as she could, and fortunately George did not follow. "Bryan, come with me!" She glanced over her shoulder at her older son, but he didn't move from his sire's side, even though she could see the lad's legs trembling. He held firm.

She wanted to go back. She wanted to rip him from his father's side, but she feared George would stop her from leaving.

"Bryan, please!" she shouted again, desperate. But he shook his head silently. And so she kept running, driven forward by Brice's screams.

They were joined in the woods by other women with the same goal.

Living.

"Mama! They're using big swords," Brice said, his voice choked by tears.

She found a group of thick bushes to hide in. Making her way inside, she knew there were brambles, but she thought it looked to be the safest place.

"Mama, they're pricking me," her lad whimpered.

"Aye, they will, but we'll not notice them anymore when we're in the middle—and they'll prick anyone who comes near us." When she thought they were well hidden, she sat cross-legged in the dry earth and settled Brice on her lap, hugging him tight to her bosom. Then she prayed for Bryan. For Brice. And for all of them.

Brice sniffled, and she kissed his forehead and whispered, "Try not to make a sound, lad. We dinnae want them to hear us. What would ye like for dinner on the morrow?"

That distracted him enough for him to whisper his favorites to her—lamb meat pie or a big bowl of porridge with honey. She listened for evidence of the knights moving past them—*oh, please, let them just be passing by*—but it didn't come.

Instead, they were battered by sounds of metal clashing, shouts of anger, yelps of pain, and bellows of violent battle, the sounds coming closer and closer, enough so that she covered Brice's ears and entreated him to close his eyes.

She peeked through the brambles of the brush and caught sight of George not far away, fighting two men at once. Desperate for a glimpse of Bryan, she looked all around, shifting slightly for a better vantage point, but she didn't see him. Her heart nearly wrenched in two. Where was her eldest son?

George shouted two words at the top of his voice as he swung his small sword with one hand and his dagger with the other, but he took a sword to his belly. A scream attempted to push past Cara's lips, but she bit it back, her son's safety foremost on her mind. Her husband clutched the wound, looking at the blood on his tunic while his attackers chuckled. One kicked him over with a boot, and both of them left to fight others.

How she wanted to go to him, but she held fast to her son, who hadn't seen his father go down, thank God. He'd closed his eyes, just as she'd told him, his sobs drowned out by the screams of battle.

Her hands were still over his ears, and so he hadn't heard his father's last words.

But *she* had.

"Cara, fight!"

It had happened so quickly. Two of the men they'd sent ahead to patrol while they finished their meal had come back to their ranks. "My lord, there is a group of six huts we're almost upon in front of a deserted castle. They're directly in our path to Bothwell. Shall we engage or pass them by?"

Hepple had thought it over for a moment, pacing in his nervous way, his hands behind his back. He rarely held still, his hands, his fingers, or his feet were always moving, probably one of the reasons he stayed so slender. His brown hair had thinned remarkably, but he kept it long and tethered. "Did you see any young women?"

"Aye, my lord. Several went into hiding."

"Take as many knights as you need and kill the men. Leave the women and children alive so I can check them. Do the deed. We'll be along in half of the hour."

The knights had departed, taking ten others with them. Gabriel had ordered the others to pack up and be ready to leave in ten minutes, should the others require any assistance. But he'd struggled to concentrate on anything but the bloodlust he saw in Hepple. The baron's twisted grin had sickened him.

What had made him think he could handle being a part of this war between the Scots and the English? War between men he understood, but not this.

Not harming innocents. His predecessor, it was whispered, had been hung and left for the buzzards—a punishment he'd suffered due to a simple disagreement with Hepple. If Gabriel tried to stop the killing of the women and children, he'd be slaughtered. He might not get his chance to avenge Della and follow through on his plan, but at least he'd get to see her again. Hold her in his arms.

Perhaps it was time to end this fruitless endeavor of his.

It was then he'd decided what he would do. He'd defend the women and children and likely be struck down because of it. He'd take his last breath and return to the arms of his wife.

A strange calmness fell over him as he mounted his horse. Hepple had gone ahead of him. He hoped his attempt would save the life of at least one child, and if he were as strong a fighter as he thought he was, he'd take a couple of knights along with him.

By the time they neared the small village, the screams had died down to the mutterings of those nearly dead, lying on the ground and bleeding. He said a small prayer to ease the dead's suffering. He understood war and the costs.

But it was wrong to involve women and children, and for that, he would take a stand.

He reached the lane that ran through the village, doing his best to ignore the cries of the wounded, and searched out the women and children.

The survivors were lined up at the end of the

lane. Four women. A few children. The rest had probably been sent away.

Hepple was moving from female to female, assessing each of them for their suitability to his needs.

One woman stood in the middle, two boys gathered in front of her. Hepple was standing before her, instructing her to open her mouth so he could check her teeth. She wore a necklace that caught his eye, the blue stone winking up at him as if he'd seen it before.

Something strange came over him in that moment—almost as if an aura surrounded the woman that was drawing him closer. Without quite intending to, he dismounted and made his way through the knights until he stood next to Hepple.

But he couldn't take his gaze off the beautiful woman. Something about her reminded him of his Della. Her hair was red and her eyes green, unlike Della, who'd had brown hair and brown eyes, but he saw the resemblance in the defiant lift of her chin. In the haunting look in her eyes as she clutched her two sons to her skirts.

Hepple reached up and cupped her breast, and the woman swung her hand at him. The baron grabbed her wrist, preventing the slap from landing, and reached for the roots of her hair. He yanked her forward, but she didn't make a sound, instead pursing her lips to control the pain he was surely causing her.

Just like Della would have.

The baron hissed, a wee bit of spittle leaving his lips. "If I want to feel the merchandise, I will. Perhaps I'll decide I'd like to see more and have you strip down in front of all of us. Would you like that, you haughty miss?"

She gritted her teeth and said nothing, while Hepple's clenched jaw told Gabriel he was about to strike her. The bastard swung out to slap her cheek, but Gabriel caught his hand. "Leave her be," he growled. "Her sons are watching."

The look Hepple gave him might have made a lesser man wither, but Gabriel held his ground, tightening his grip on the man's wrist. He stared back at the man with all the contempt and anger he felt toward him. After a moment, something else appeared in the baron's gaze—fear.

To his surprise, Hepple stepped back, releasing her.

"Fine. She's in your charge. She's the one I want, but you will control her. We take the boys as assurance that she'll do as we ask. Now get them out of my sight. Meet me at Bothwell Castle by midnight."

And with that one move, his entire world changed.

Would it be for the better?

Or for worse?

CHAPTER THREE

С ARA HAD WISHED TO KICK and scratch the bastard who had mauled her and yanked her out of the bushes, but she'd had a protector. The question was, why?

Once the man in charge had relinquished her and her sons to the taller man, their protector had led the three of them back to their hut. Neither lad had said anything, Bryan's face still tear-stained from watching his father die in battle. One of the knights had taken pity on him, thank God, and sent him to wait near the forest. Now he clung to her, something quite unusual for him.

"Pack your things. One bag for you. One for the boys. You'll follow me on horseback," the tall man said. "I'll take one of your sons with me to guarantee you'll not try to escape."

Cara hastened to grab their things, knowing it was unusual to be given such an opportunity, but Bryan quickly stepped forward, glancing at his younger brother. "I'll go with ye."

A moment passed, and the tall man shook his head. "I'll take the younger one." He looked at

Cara, seeing she was done. "We leave now."

Not another word was spoken. He hurriedly moved them out, leading them past the remaining survivors, who'd been tied up and were being hustled back into their huts. She hated to imagine what their fate would be, but she'd heard the stories. They all had. Even if they were left alive, they wouldn't survive for long without any men to fight off the marauders running rampant around their land. What was wrong with King Edward that he had ordered such senseless slaughter? Not thinking about their fate would serve her better than dwelling on it. For now, she had two sons to protect.

Although she feared to learn why they had been spared.

The man in charge had given them two horses from those taken from the village. Once they were on horseback, the tall man headed away from the group of knights. He'd settled her youngest, Brice, in front of him. Bryan rode with her. She might have tried to escape with Brice, hoping Bryan would escape on his own, but she would never leave her youngest. The man's perceptiveness surprised her.

It would make him a stronger adversary.

The air was cool for spring, but she had her mantle wrapped tightly around her.

"Where are we going?" she finally asked.

"You don't need to know. It will take us half a day. You'll find out then. Your name?"

"Cara."

"The lads and their ages?" he asked gruffly.

"Bryan is eight summers. Brice is with ye and he is five. And yer name?"

He turned his head to stare at her as if pondering whether to be truthful. "Gabriel. That's all you need to know."

"Mama, I'm scared," Brice called out to her.

"Ye must be strong. If Lord Gabriel had meant to hurt us, he would have done so already. He will be yer friend."

As if an Englishman could ever be a friend.

Brice turned around to peer up at the man behind him, who continued to stare straight ahead. Then, to her surprise, the man patted her son's head lightly.

She hadn't taken his measure until now. Stricken by horror and frightened for her lads' lives, she'd only noticed that he was at least a head taller than the baron and weighed probably twice as much— all of it muscle. His shoulders and upper arms were massive, bigger than she'd ever seen on a man before.

That she'd assessed early on. What she hadn't assessed before was how pleasing his appearance was to the eye. His hair was a dark brown, mostly straight but curled up at his shoulders. He had a moustache and beard, but he kept them trimmed instead of long and ragged as many did. She hadn't noticed the color of his eyes yet, but she would take note when she had the chance.

Why had he made the move to protect her? What did it mean?

"What are they going to do with the others?"

she asked, even though she'd decided she'd be better off not knowing.

"I don't know, and in war, I'll give a piece of advice, my lady. Don't ask questions if you suspect you won't like the answer."

That was their only conversation on the trip that did indeed take half the day. Brice had fallen asleep against Gabriel, and to her surprise, he actually arranged the lad so he was more comfortable.

The sun was nearly dropping by the time they advanced on a manor home well hidden from the main path. Neatly kept, it appeared deserted. She waited until they arrived before she said anything.

Lord Gabriel settled Brice on the ground and ordered Bryan to dismount, which he did immediately. "Which sack is theirs?"

She pointed and he grabbed it, handing it to Bryan.

When she attempted to dismount on her own, the man spun on his heel and ground out, "Not you. You'll stay. I'll explain upon my return, but if I have to chase you, it will be the lads who suffer, not you."

Turning toward her sons, he said, "Say goodbye to your mama. She has a job to do, then she'll be back."

She had no idea what he meant by that, but she wouldn't ask him in front of them.

No matter what, she couldn't let her tears fall. Brice would cry if she did. "You lads be good and I'll return for ye as soon as I'm able." Shifting her gaze to her eldest son, she added, "Bryan, take care of yer brother."

"Come, boys, there are puppies inside." Gabriel pointed to the house, his expression warning them not to delay any longer.

"Puppies?" Brice asked, sounding excited, if only for a moment. "Bye, Mama."

Bryan said, "I'll watch over him, Mama. Come back soon." She could see in his posture that he hesitated to leave her. Proud of the young lad he was becoming, she thanked the Lord again for him. Bryan would indeed watch over Brice.

She said, "Go see the puppies with Brice." The two boys hurried after Gabriel without another word.

No other threat would ensure her compliance, and surely he knew it. He returned in a short time later, grabbing the reins of her horse and leading her away from the house. After throwing a glance past her shoulder, he returned his gaze to her. "Now, listen well and heed my words. You are a prisoner of King Edward, and you were taken to perform as a spy for him. You will do as you're told, or the boys will suffer. If you do well, you will be granted supervised visits with them. I tell you this now because you need to consider my words and accept them before we get to Bothwell Castle, our final destination. If you argue with the baron, your boys will pay and so will you. I give you this time to learn to accept your situation."

"May I know who is caring for them?"

"You may not, but they are in the hands of some-one I trust completely. I wouldn't leave innocent children with just anyone. Be glad I got to choose where they are being kept. If the baron had made the decision, they'd be in the dungeons at Bothwell Castle.

She opened her mouth to speak but closed it again.

"Wise lady. You have no say in this. You will ride with me so I don't have to chase you down should you foolishly try to escape. I tell you this now because if you wish to argue with your fate, you'd do best to argue with me. You won't wish to see the repercussions of your arguments after we arrive at the castle. You've already seen the baron's ways. He is not a kind or patient man."

"I hope there are truly puppies inside."

"There are. I'm not a liar, my lady." He took his horse and led it to the small stable behind the home before returning to her, checking the area before leading her horse off the property.

He mounted behind her and she sat straight up, refusing to touch him. Her mind jumped in a thousand directions as he sent his horse into a canter, shifting into a gallop once they hit a meadow.

A spy. She was to be used as a spy against her people. And if she refused to turn traitor, they would kill or torture her boys. The futility of her situation fell over her like the most ominous cloud ever. Her husband was dead, and her sons were being held captive.

Would she ever see her sons again?

*

Cara was a stronger woman than Gabriel would have guessed. He'd expected sobs and pleas for mercy, but all he'd heard were a few sniffles that ended quickly.

She'd done her best to ride with her spine as straight as the blade of his sword, but he'd encouraged her to relax. "If you stay like that for the whole ride, you won't be able to move by nightfall. If you hear anything I say, it's that you'll need your strength and your wits to make it through for your lads. This is war and you're a part of it now."

She'd stayed strong for another ten minutes, but then she'd sagged against him, an audible sigh releasing from her.

He did his best to ignore the curves of the beauty leaning against him. She was quite stunning. Her green eyes promised to bewitch a man if he got too close. Her beauty had probably saved her life and her sons' lives.

He would do what he could to protect them. His vow to stop all the killing had changed as soon as he'd seen those little lads at her skirts, all of them with the same arresting green eyes.

Della was to have a son. *Their* son, but it wasn't to be.

His gut had told him it was paramount to protect these three, and so he had abandoned his plan. He had no idea what had happened to the other survivors, but he didn't wish to know either.

He found a small clearing not far from a burn, so he stopped. First, he led his horse to the water, then he found him a spot where he could feed on the tall grasses of spring. The animal's chomping was the only sound to be heard besides the occasional hoot of an owl and the scampering of the red squirrels in the trees. It would be a good place to speak with her.

"Take care of your needs. Please don't try to run instead. If you do, I'll surely catch you since you are on foot and I have the horse. If that were to happen, all your future needs will be taken care of in front of me. I don't know many lasses who would appreciate that."

She regarded him with a stony expression. "Truthfully, I'm too exhausted to run. But don't discount that it could happen on the morrow." She stepped toward a group of bushes, then glanced back at him and said, "Ye want honesty, I'll give it to ye. I'd do anything for my lads."

He couldn't help but grin. He liked feisty women. Much like Della.

He forced himself not to think about her. It was still too painful.

Cara came back around the bushes, a small blush evident on her cheeks. He turned his back to her, giving her a moment of privacy, and said, "We'll eat quickly, then continue on toward the castle. I'll not sleep here and take the chance of being set upon by marauders." He grabbed a package of dried meat from his satchel to share and handed her an apple and the skin he'd filled with fresh water from the burn.

He pointed to a flat rock and said, "Sit. You need to hear what I have to say."

She did as he asked and bit into the apple, chewing it slowly, her gaze never leaving his.

"We will stay at Bothwell Castle for a short time, then I suspect you will be sent to Edinburgh to spy."

Her response was quick. "Who will we be spying on and just exactly how am I to do this?" She swiped at a trickle of apple juice at the corner of her mouth.

He had a sudden urge to lick that juice himself.

Fool. She lost her husband this day. She hates you.

He gave her an honest answer. "I'm not exactly sure. You are aware that King Edward wishes to control all of Scotland himself. He has already taken many areas in the Borderlands and the Lowlands in England's name, slaughtering many Scots along the way. I'm curious as to why the men in your village decided to stay instead of heading into the Highlands as others have done." He stopped, lifting an eyebrow to see if she would agree with that statement. He took a seat on another rock close by, allowing him the chance to see her. "I take it one of them was your husband? If so, my sympathies for your loss."

"My husband knew 'twas possible we'd be attacked, aye, but he thought we could fight ye. We'd heard that yer warriors were weak from lack of food, so he thought we had a chance." She stared at the ground at her feet, a small tear escaping one eye before she quickly swiped it away.

"That was true of the men traveling with King Edward, but not our men. Our number is small compared to the large number he led. We ate well and brought much with us in the expectation that we were to hold Bothwell Castle in the king's name."

"That doesnae explain why ye need my assistance."

"King Edward has demanded that the remaining Scots swear fealty to him. Many have done so willingly, and others will continue to travel to Edinburgh or Berwick Castle to make the pledge. Being a suspicious monarch, he doesn't trust that all of the Scots are being honest. He is fully aware of the work of William Wallace and Robert Bruce, and he is also aware of the failings of King John. Our charge is to see which Scots are truly supportive of King Edward and which are lying through their teeth."

"So I must spy on my brethren? How will I do this? I don't know any but the ones in our small village."

"You will travel to Edinburgh Castle with someone, though I know not who yet, and then you will flirt your way into gaining your brethren's trust." A fire lit in her eyes at that, but she was wise enough not to speak. "If you get caught in any lies, you will lose your life and probably your sons as well. Is it harsh? Most definitely, but don't doubt that Baron Hepple will see it through." He ran his hand through his thick hair, debating how truthful he should be, how much she could handle. Since her sons' lives were at stake, he decided she deserved the complete truth.

"Hepple is reputed to be one of the cruelest barons in England. I suspect this is why he was chosen for the task. Do as you're told or you'll all die."

CHAPTER FOUR

THEY ARRIVED AT BOTHWELL CASTLE shortly after midnight. Cara had said little to the man behind her on the horse, the reality of her situation sinking into her. Utterly exhausted, she could barely sit the horse for the remainder of their journey.

As they moved toward the gate, Gabriel whispered in her ear. "I suggest you trust no one here. If you must go to someone, it should be me. As you have already seen, I am the only one who will offer you protection."

She couldn't help but ask the question that had been foremost in her mind all day. "And why is that?"

"Because I am one of the few who believes women and children should not suffer from the tragedies and cruelties of men's wars. I will have your sons' best interests at heart. While I don't know all the others here, most of them do not share my conviction. Keep that in mind while you're here. I know not where I will be sent once we step inside the castle walls."

He set her down from the horse with a gentle

touch for which she was grateful. Her legs nearly buckled underneath her, but he caught her and set her upright after he jumped from his mount. He took the horse to the stable and said, "Wait here."

She did as he asked, her arms wrapped around herself against the cold wind. The curtain wall looked monstrous, but it wasn't finished. Either that or her eyes played tricks on her. At one corner of the wall sat a huge tower unlike anything she'd ever seen, and the curtain wall spanned from the large tower to a smaller tower farther away.

There was no keep in the middle, just that massive tower, and not much of the curtain wall had been completed. She lifted her gaze to the top of the tower. An odd feeling came over her as the low clouds moved quickly over the half moon, casting an eerie darkness over the entire place. Numb. She felt numb and full of dread and worry.

Men shuffled about outside of the castle, but there weren't many of them. Most were probably resting.

Rest.

Aye, she needed to sleep and then she could make a plan of some sort. Judging from the horses milling about, there were too many men here for her to fight her way to freedom. Her best plan would probably be to travel to Edinburgh Castle and attempt to meet up with a true Scot who could help her. George's brother had gone to the Highlands. Someone would know where to find him, and if she'd find a way to get to one of the large Highland clans, she'd have protection from the English, something she expected would be necessary for many moons to come.

But nothing could happen until she found her boys again. She'd done her best to try to memorize where they'd been left, paying attention to the sun and any landmarks they passed, but after a while it had all become a blur in the dark.

She suspected it was one of the reasons they'd traveled in the dark, to keep her from knowing exactly where they were being kept.

Gabriel returned and set his hand on her lower back. "I was told by the stable master that I am to take you to your chamber at the top of the tower. You will remain there for the few days you are here, and you are fortunate enough to have a few small windows for you to see the countryside. You will stay in your chamber until summoned. I'm to stay with you and keep watch." He grabbed their two bags and led her to the tower.

She said nothing but followed along. There were too many guards casting lascivious looks her way for her to object. She moved closer to Gabriel. He hadn't touched her inappropriately yet, and he'd had plenty of opportunity, so she had to assume he was far safer than any of the other knights or warriors presently roaming around Bothwell Castle.

Once inside, they moved up the winding staircase along the outside of the larger tower, ignoring the men sleeping in the chamber at the base of the stairs. The higher they climbed, the tighter her grip became on Gabriel's tunic, until he turned back toward her and took her hand, leading her up the staircase. They passed at least two other levels, although she couldn't see inside the chambers. They finally reached the top, and he opened the door. She was surprised to see two large connected chambers, separated by a door that was currently open. The front one had a hearth and a table surrounded by six chairs, while the other had a large bed with curtains around it, a small hearth on the outside wall, and various chests for storage and chairs for sitting.

There was only one bed, but a small pallet sat close to the hearth. She turned to look at Gabriel, waiting to see what he would say.

He pointed outside the chambers at the garderobe in the small area at the top of the stairs. "Use it and I'll keep watch. Then you may have the bed, and I'll sleep on the floor in the chamber with the table, directly in front of your door, so no one will bother you."

"But…" She didn't know how to offer him anything else. She was exhausted down to her bones and she would never be able to sleep on the floor.

He set a finger to her lips and said, "Use the garderobe. I'll put your bag inside your chamber. If there's no fresh water for your use, I'll find some. Once you're refreshed, go to sleep on the bed, close the door, and I'll check on you in the morn."

She did as he asked, then made her way into the bedchamber, closing the door and leaning against it. After a moment, she found herself thinking of the battle from earlier. The violence. The look in George's eyes as he shouted at her to fight. The cold-blooded violence with which those men had attacked the villagers. What if the English soldiers got up to her chamber? What would they do?

She whirled around and opened the door, surprised to see Gabriel arranging his sword near him. He'd gathered some blankets and furs on the floor.

"What?" he asked, peering at her from his spot on the floor.

"Naught. I just wished to see where ye were sleeping."

"Here, as I said. I'll not move from this spot. I promise."

She nodded, then whispered, "Many thanks to ye." Somehow she owed him. She knew it. He might be the enemy, but he had helped her and her sons.

She closed the door and slid the lock into position, checked it twice, then moved over to warm her hands at the small fire in the hearth. Noticing the furs over the window, she pulled them back to peer out over the countryside, surprised to see the light of the moon reflecting off the water of a nearby river. She had no idea which one, but she would wager it was quite a view in the sunlight.

For now, she needed sleep more than anything.

She removed her boots and mantle, and lifted the covers on the bed, pleased to see there were several furs to keep her warm.

She no longer had a husband to warm her or any wee bodies to snuggle with her in the cold morn.

Once her head settled on the pillow, she finally shed a few tears.

But by all that was holy, she'd not be shedding any more tears on the morrow.

She had two lads who were depending on her to be strong.

❧

It was well past dawn when she awakened the next morn. She rubbed the sleep from her eyes and opened her door carefully, planning to head directly to the garderobe. And then she saw him.

She'd opened the door so quietly that Gabriel hadn't heard her. He was cleaning his face and upper body by a basin on the table, his back to her. And what a back it was...

The man was magnificent. Her mouth went dry as she watched. The more he moved, the more his muscles rippled across his back, the water dripping over his shoulder as he scrubbed under his arm.

What was wrong with her? This man was holding her captive and she was admiring his back and, if she had to admit it, his finely honed backside. She coughed lightly, not wishing to let on that she'd been staring, and he spun around. "Your pardon, my lord, but I must use the garderobe."

His voice husky, his eyes dark, he said, "Do as you must."

His chest was even more magnificent than his back, the dark hairs leading her gaze from the top down to the flat plane of his belly. One glance at this powerful man on display in front of her sent heat straight to the place between her thighs, something that was not in her control at all. It was an instinctive reaction that appalled and embarrassed her. She pulled her gaze away, but not before she saw the small smile appear on his features. He'd caught her staring, and she wished to run away. What was wrong with her? How could she react so inappropriately toward her captor?

Because she'd never seen such an impressive specimen of a man before, and she doubted she'd ever see his like again.

He followed her out the door, and she slipped into the garderobe while he made his way down to the next level. She heard him giving orders for water to be brought up, though she didn't catch any the specifics. When she finished, she made her way back into the bedchamber and washed her hands in her own basin, doing her best to straighten the rumpled gown she'd slept in.

When he entered, he nodded to her. "I have ordered a tub bath for you, my lady. The tub will be brought up as soon as the water is heated. Hopefully, you've brought another gown to don. Be ready to greet the baron in an hour. He will go over your instructions." He stepped forward and touched his hand to hers for a brief moment before he dropped it. "Do your best to be agreeable. I know not what he has planned yet, but we'll find out soon enough."

She took her time in the tub because it was a luxury she rarely had. Settling into the warm water was heavenly. If only the rest of her new world could disappear. It took her a bit of time to dry her hair in front of the fire, and she left it down because it was still damp when she heard the knock on the door.

"Come in," she said, standing.

Gabriel looked at her a moment before speaking, some emotion flickering through his eyes. "The baron is here, my lady," he said. "Please join us at the table."

She finished brushing her hair and made her way to the table, not speaking to anyone.

The baron reached for her hair. She pulled back, instantly regretting that she'd worn it down, but he still managed to run his fingers through the very end of her strands.

"My, your dark red hair is quite beautiful. I think you'll work out quite nicely."

Her only response was to swing her hair over her shoulder to avoid his touch. The baron glared at her and began to pace while Gabriel took the chair next to her.

"You have left the boys in a safe place?" He directed this question to Gabriel. How she wished she had any idea where they were being kept or who cared for them. Although she'd seen the manor, she didn't know how to get back to it.

"Aye, they are well cared for." Gabriel didn't mince words with the baron, to her surprise. He apparently didn't like being questioned.

The controlling man paced a few more times before stopping in quite a dramatic pose, his hands behind his back and his chin lifted. The effect was undermined by the fact that the hair on his head needing washing and his beard was in desperate need of trimming, unlike Gabriel's finely trimmed dark beard.

"You will leave for Edinburgh today. Both of you. You will present yourselves as a married couple, the Mac Henrys from the Lowlands. You've both sworn fealty to King Edward and are arriving to make it formal. You, my dear, will make yourself available to other men so you can engage them in a level of intimacy that will encourage them to trust and confide in you. Are they loyal to our king or are they lying? This is what I wish to know. I also expect that the Scots are gathering somewhere when they leave the Lowlands. You are to find out where they're going and inform me as soon as possible. You will go for one sennight, then you are to return to me with all the information you have gathered. You will tell me everything, and I will send the important information along to King Edward."

She glanced at Gabriel to see if he would react to this dictate, but he didn't say anything. He left her with no choice but to speak directly to the baron. "Excuse me, my lord. What level of intimacy are ye referring to? I dinnae understand."

He leaned down and placed his face so close to hers that their noses nearly touched. "You're not a virgin, so do as you must to gain the information if you wish to ever see your sons again. Do I make myself clear?"

She gasped and leaned back, shocked at his insinuation. "Will my boys be returned to me after the sennight?" No matter how awful the situation, she would do what it took to see her lads again. "And will we be allowed to leave? There would be no reason for me to return once we've sworn fealty."

"That is for me to decide. More Scots will continue to arrive so I may choose to send you back. Just remember that you will do as I ask and nothing more. Or less."

Gabriel pushed her knee under the table. She glanced at him and he gave her a glare that warned her to be quiet.

The baron paced again, then he paused by the window, a small smile twisting his lips. "If you would prefer, you could be my mistress for the sennight instead. Would that be more to your liking, my dear?"

It took every bit of inner strength and fortitude she possessed not to react to that comment. What an outrageous proposition. She couldn't speak at all, her mind reeling from all the outrages that had been heaped on her at once.

Ultimately, though, she knew she had no choice. "I will go with Gabriel and do as ye wish. Then I expect to see my lads, as ye promised."

She would not stay here with Baron Hepple. Anything but the baron.

"My lord," Gabriel said. "We'll pack and leave in two hours. I will meet with you after we break our fast for any further instructions."

"As you wish," the baron responded. He approached Cara then, reaching forward and running his finger down her jawline. She did something she instantly regretted.

She bit him.

The resounding slap across her cheek from him made her see stars.

"Montgomerie, you'd better control your charge." He held his finger up to peruse the damage.

Gabriel bolted from his chair. "I will. She's been through a major shock losing her husband and her sons. I ask you to consider that when you deliberate over her punishment."

The baron narrowed his gaze on her. "If she's still here in two hours, she'll come to my chamber and I'll see her duly punished. If you're wise, you'll get her away as soon as you can. I'm losing patience with her, but we must heed the king's command."

From the look in his eyes, Cara did not wish to learn what kind of punishment he would choose for her. It was time to go.

CHAPTER FIVE

GABRIEL FEARED HIS HEAD WOULD explode, but he held back until the baron departed.

He stared at the door, listening to the sounds of the man's departure, then turned back to glare at Cara. "Are you out of your mind? Why would you bite the man who had your husband killed and your lads locked away?"

"I dinnae know. I dinnae like him touching me." Her hands fisted at her sides, the whiteness of her knuckles clearly visible do him, reminding him of how much she'd been through the day before.

Still, he felt it his duty to keep her safe, though he had no idea where that compulsion had originated. "He can do whatever he wishes. He has an army of over fifty knights outside this castle. I suggest you not push him any further. Pack your things, do what you must, but we're leaving within the hour before you get us both killed."

"Can we no' eat first? I'm starving. I had barely anything to eat at all."

Struck by the dark circles under her eyes, by the

way she now kneaded her hands together, and the fear in her gaze, he relented. Perhaps he was being too harsh. He'd do best to remember what he'd just told the baron—her husband had been killed, her children taken.

She mumbled what she must have considered to be an apology. "It was just a reaction. I dinnae think on it before I did it. Clearly, I did no' think at all." Then she did the oddest thing. She stuck her tongue out and swiped it with a linen square. "I shouldnae have done it. It feels like I can taste him now."

She moved her tongue back and forth so much that he was hard in an instant. What the devil was this lass about? Did she not know what she was doing or how that sweet little tongue would affect a man?

Hellfire, he had to get out. "I'm going for food. Pack your things."

"I never unpacked," she whispered.

"Then sit there and don't move from this chamber. Could you please?"

Her reply was to roll her eyes, but she softened it with a nod. She got up and moved over to the hearth, warming her hands, so he left.

When he stepped into the stairwell, he took a moment to gather his wits. Hellfire, but this woman would be the death of him yet. What the hell had he been thinking when he'd made the decision to protect her and her boys?

Sweat broke out across his brow as he thought of what it would mean to act the part of her husband.

He'd be forced to stand next to her, choose her food with that wee tongue darting out, help her down from her horse. Those small actions would all add up to a serious assault on his senses. The only solution was to don a plaid to hide his ever-growing traitorous member whenever she was around. The red strands falling around her face had begged to be caressed, just as the porcelain skin of her neck beseeched him to taste the salt of her skin.

He'd been too long without a woman. That was the problem. Perhaps he should find himself a woman to relieve him of his cravings as soon as they arrived in Edinburgh.

That was it. He had no other choice but to find a woman to slake the insatiable lust coursing through his body. The decision made, he headed down to the stables first to advise the lads to ready a horse within the hour, though he had to pinch the bridge of his nose to stop the memory of her soft backside rubbing against him.

He was doomed to purgatory—a throbbing manhood from here until Edinburgh.

He stopped in the kitchen, then returned to the tower chamber with a tray of food—porridge in two bowls, a small bowl of honey, goat's milk, and two slices of bread. "Eat up, then we leave."

They ate in silence.

When they'd nearly finished, she stared at her bowl and whispered, "How do I do this? He has asked me to whore for information. I dinnae know if I can."

He understood her concern. The poor woman

had probably only been with one man in her whole life, and she'd only been a widow for a day. "We'll talk about this more in Edinburgh, but I don't see it as whoring necessarily." He considered his words carefully.

Her gaze lifted to him, a burst of hope in her lovely eyes. "Ye do no'?"

"Nay, I believe you can tantalize a man with a kiss or two. Can you consider kissing a few men? Flirting with them? Many a man will spill everything he knows if the right woman brushes against them with her curves. A far cry from whoring, in my opinion, but understand I am not a woman when I make that statement."

He waited to see how she would react to his words. Her eyes widened, then she stared at the far wall, considering the implications. He admired the way she approached the difficult position they'd put her in. Rather than simper or shed tears, she sought to understand her predicament in order to consider her best alternatives.

She turned back to him and asked, "A man would reveal secrets to a woman who brushed her upper body against him? 'Tis all that's needed?"

The seriousness in her expression told him she had no idea of her beauty or her ability to attract a man. "Many a man would tell *all* his secrets for the attentions of a beautiful woman such as yourself."

She stared at him, pondering the statement. He watched the emotions flit across her gaze— confusion, uncertainty, disbelief even. "You don't consider yourself beautiful, do you?" he whispered.

She shook her head and blushed. How he wished he could see how far that blush traveled. Would it travel over her whole body or stop at her neck? Perhaps her breasts, possibly turning her nipples a duskier shade of...

Of what? Pink? Coral? Or would they be a rich shade of brown?

"Your husband never told you that you were beautiful? He didn't make love to you every night just to hold you in his arms, share his heat with you, caress your skin the way he should to give you pleasure?"

She shook her head and bolted out of her seat, nearly toppling her chair over. Rushing to the window, she yanked the fur back and stuck her head out into the cool air.

If he had to guess, he'd say the woman had never experienced an orgasm. "Your husband wasn't a loving man," he said gently. "I take it he did not appreciate what he had."

She glanced over her shoulder at him with a stunned look, then shifted her attention back to the window.

He'd learned some valuable information about Cara Breckenridge, soon to be Mac Henry. If he had his way, he'd protect her, protect her sons.

And he'd have her shouting his name as she plunged over the edge of ecstasy.

He had a new goal in his life.

Cara had to admit she'd been afraid of what

would happen on their ride after the indecent conversation they'd shared at Bothwell Castle. But fortunately Gabriel made last-minute arrangements with the stablemaster to give her a horse of her own.

"I don't wish to overburden them on the ride to Edinburgh," he explained. "We'll not stop unless absolutely necessary and should arrive before nightfall."

Still, she didn't know what to make of his words. George had been a good provider and a wonderful father to their boys.

But he'd never called her beautiful. That word didn't belong with her name, not in her eyes. Her lips were too big, her hair had too much curl, and she wished her breasts were smaller. They'd grown when she'd fed her boys, but they'd never returned to the smaller size they'd been before she had carried.

George had wanted them smaller, too. Another way she felt she'd failed her husband.

And Gabriel's comment about her husband making love to her every night, holding her in his arms? That was almost laughable. Some nights she had longed to be wrapped in his heat, but he'd always preferred to sleep without touching her.

She'd adjusted.

The truth was she mourned the loss of her laddies more than her husband, and that made her ashamed.

What was wrong with her?

When they arrived in Edinburgh, Gabriel

motioned for her to follow him to the stables on the outskirts of town. She couldn't take her gaze off the imposing view of the massive royal castle. A huge curtain wall with several towers surrounded a large keep that overlooked the entire city. Larger than any structure she'd ever seen, it sat high up on a hill. It seemed too large and magnificent to be real, something created in her mind in a dream.

She'd never seen so many people bustling about in one place. And the smells were less than wonderful. Horses, pigs, nearly every kind of animal could be seen in pens near the outskirts of town, their stench carrying into the paths of the peasants walking or riding through the village.

"Are we no' headed to the castle?" she asked as she did her best to guide her horse around passersby.

"Nay, we go to the main portion of the city. We need a tailor. Both of us are lacking in proper clothing for the royal castle. We must play our parts."

She didn't ask any other questions, her eyes fixed on all the sights of the city. When they reached the stables and Gabriel helped her dismount, he said, "'Tis late. We'll stay in the inn across the road and we'll visit the tailor in the morn."

Nodding, she followed him. She knew nothing of this world, having spent her entire life inside Breckenridge Castle as a young lass before marrying George and moving to the village outside its gates. Her father had worked in the armory and her mother had baked for the laird, earning them a cottage inside the bailey. Her only sister had married and moved away long ago, and her parents had left with the laird's family, heading to the Highlands when Edward started ravaging the Borderlands.

She had no idea where they were now. They'd begged George to come with them, and his brother had issued invitation after invitation, too, but he'd refused everyone, saying he knew best. He'd been a stubborn man, for sure. Had they left for the Highlands, he might still be alive, and she probably would not be in her present predicament. It was hard to be upset with him when he'd lost his life, but she did harbor some anger over what could have been.

They were about to step inside the small building when Gabriel stopped and said, "Remember the ruse. You are Cara Mac Henry, my wife, and I am Lord Mac Henry to you. We're from Perthshire."

The inn was larger than any of the cottages in her ruined village, and it looked to be as tall as it was wide. The door opened directly into the dining hall, and a few people still sat at the tables enjoying their meal. Her stomach rumbled over the smell of stew, and she hung her head in embarrassment, hoping he'd not heard it over the small din of chatter about them.

He motioned for her to precede him to the desk at the back of the hall. "My lady and I are in need of a room for one night," he said, making his way to the innkeeper.

The man was middle-aged, trim, and quite serious. The woman who stood behind him, his wife, if she had to guess, was plain but pleasant, wearing a wide smile. "We'll be pleased to have ye," he said with a nod. He reached for a key, then led them upstairs to a room at the end of the passageway, not overlooking the dining hall, for which she was grateful.

"Ye'll find good linens on the bed, plenty of furs. Will ye join us for something to eat, my lord?" he asked, stepping back as he opened the door and handed Gabriel the key.

"If ye could send two bowls of stew to us, we'd be pleased with yer hospitality. And a loaf of yer finest bread and two ales." He handed a few coins to the innkeeper, who nodded and left.

Cara arched her eyebrows at Gabriel and gave him a slight smile. "Ye slipped into a Scottish brogue quite easily, my lord."

"Aye, 'tis no' so difficult, as ye ken see. How heavy shall I make me brogue?" he asked, smiling back at her. "My mother was Scottish, but my father lived in England near the Borderlands before they married. I'm quite used to both tongues."

"Ye've been around the Scots too much," she said, removing her mantle. To her surprise, he grabbed it up and hung it on a hook near the door. She glanced around, surprised by the coziness of the chamber. There were even soft cushions on the chairs surrounding the table. The hearth was small, but Gabriel threw more logs into the fire to heat the space up quickly.

"Where are ye from?" she asked, giving in to

curiosity.

"I lived in the Borderlands, the English side."

Once the food arrived, they settled at the table to eat. After a few moments, she cleared her throat and asked, "How will we sleep in one bed? I know we must stay in the same room in order to pull off the ruse, but exactly…"

"You may sleep in the bed. I'll sleep on the floor again."

While she felt badly about it, she didn't wish to sleep on the floor. "My thanks for yer kind consideration," she whispered. There was a small partition hiding the view of the bed from the door—a small detail for which she was grateful.

She fell into bed shortly after they finished eating, exhausted after a long day of riding.

Lurching up in her bed in the middle of the night, she stared wide-eyed at the partition as she listened to a couple of drunken brawlers bang on the door.

"We heard there's a pretty lass inside, and we want a taste of her." Bawdy chuckles followed the sloppy admission.

A second voice said, "I saw her enter. Her pretty green eyes made it clear she wanted me. She's a beauty, that one."

The slurring of their words told her exactly what shape they were in. But at least a door separated her from them. The next sound she heard shocked her more. The whistling of a sword being unsheathed carried through the chamber—and then the door opened. "Take yerself away from the door unless ye wish to be speared by the end of my best friend here."

If she were to guess, a couple of fists were tossed about before the drunken fools took their leave. When she heard the door close again, she tiptoed out of her bed and peeked around the partition.

He stood there with no shirt on, heaving from the exertion of his small battle.

"Yer hand is bleeding."

"Foolish lads." He shook his hand, reaching for a linen square to mop up the little bit of dripping blood.

She stepped around the partition, dipped another linen in the water in the basin, and tended his hand. Standing this close to him, enveloped in his scent, she could feel the beating of her own heart. It was a pleasing aroma, one that spoke of pine branches and the outdoors, even with the sheen of sweat on his chest. Being this close to him, especially to his bare skin, unsettled her. George had never unsettled her, but perhaps that was because they'd been so familiar with each other.

Overpowered with the desire to mop the sweat from his dark chest hairs, she kept her gaze on his knuckles, pleased to see he wasn't injured badly. "My thanks again for protecting my honor. I hope they'll not bother ye again." She lifted his hand to her lips and placed a soft kiss on the worst of the abrasions. "It pleased my lads when I kissed their wounds. Forgive me if I'm too bold."

She glanced up at him, meeting brown eyes that suddenly looked darker. "It pleases me, too," he said, his voice huskier than it had been before. His other hand reached up and he ran the backs of his fingers down her cheek, a tender touch that sent butterflies afloat deep in her belly.

The moment gone, he stepped back and grabbed his sword. "I'll sleep in front of the door so they'll not bother you again."

She didn't answer, just watched him go, an odd longing filling her.

He closed the door, but then opened it enough to stick his head inside and said, "Now do ye trust in yer own appeal?"

CHAPTER SIX

GABRIEL FELT ON EDGE AS he and Cara ascended the hill on horseback toward the royal castle the next afternoon. They'd gone to the tailor, and she looked resplendent in a dark forest green gown that matched her eyes. He'd purchased another one for her on the spot, plus two more that would take the tailor some time to stitch. Judging by the look in her eyes, the two he'd ordered were more lavish than anything she'd ever worn. She looked the part, and so did he, but he kept searching the area with his gaze as they moved toward the royal castle. Always on the lookout for trouble.

It struck him that he missed the days of going to market in Berwick, when jovial bartering was the most common sound you heard, when the English and the Scots could be in the same area without fearing for their lives. When they could sit in the same inn and enjoy good food and merriment without worrying about their loved ones.

They were stopped at the gates, something Hepple had warned him would happen. "Lord Mac Henry and his wife are here for the fealty ceremony."

The guards let them inside, and a couple of stable lads hustled out to meet them. One of them assisted Cara down from her mount, then the pair of them led the horses into the stables.

"They need to be fed and brushed down," Gabriel commanded.

"Aye, my lord." The lad who answered him was no bigger than Cara's elder son. If seeing these boys made him think of her sons, he expected it would do the same to her.

One glance at her expression told him he was right. She blinked back tears, but she stayed strong, something he admired. At the door to the castle, he addressed the two guards stationed there, both dressed in fine red jackets and black trewes. "Baron Hepple sent us to swear fealty. We were advised we would be given a chamber in the royal castle. Have ye the room for the Mac Henrys?"

The guards conferred, then one said. "Aye, you will be in the west wing, my lord."

He nodded to the men, who bid them to wait while the message was conveyed to the servants. A few moments later, he and Cara were sent on their way, directed down to the end of the passageway. Once there, they were greeted by a servant who promptly took them to a private chamber. On their way to their quarters, he continued to watch their surroundings, always observant of any possible threats.

Even with her hair plaited and her body hidden under her mantle, Cara still drew many approving glances from the men who were about in the castle. An odd sense of protectiveness overcame Gabriel, compelling him to draw her closer. Was there also a touch of possessiveness in his actions?

He'd prefer not to contemplate it.

The room, when they arrived, was quite well appointed. It would appear Baron Hepple had sent a missive ahead and made special arrangements for the Mac Henrys' arrival. For this small act, he was grateful. While Cara was a beautiful woman, she was certainly a feisty one, and he had a small fear that characteristic would surface here in Edinburgh. All the better then, that they had a private space. Somewhere he could bring her if he needed to tell her to rein in her behavior.

Gabriel thanked the servant, who promptly left. Once they were safely ensconced inside, he built the fire up and fell into a chair.

Cara stood by a window overlooking the courtyard. "This chamber is enormous. 'Tis as big as our hut or larger." Dropping the heavy tapestry over the window, she took a slow turn around the chamber, admiring the furniture and décor with a touch of her hand here and there. "I had no idea how the members of royalty lived."

"All from your coin."

"I dinnae understand how that works," she said as she sidled up to him and then sat in the nearest empty chair.

"Simple, my dear. The men earn coin for their work, whatever that might be, and they pay a portion to their overlord or laird, who in turn must pay the sheriff and the king."

"But what do *they* do?" she asked, quite innocently he thought.

"The kings? They exist. Oh, they do deal with monarchs from other countries, make decisions about which products should be brought into our country, like salt or silks. Whatever strikes their fancy. Of course, they also make decisions about war. Which is what everyone fears, though it is also their responsibility to ensure the country has an army of warriors available to protect their people at any time. Of course, if they choose to wage war, it is also within their power to force all the men in the country to drop everything and join whatever fight they've started, for the betterment of the country and its people."

"But how do they know what's best for the country?"

He leaned forward and rested his elbows on the table, letting out a light chuckle. "Some kings have a talent for judging what is best. Others make terrible decisions and we must suffer the consequences."

"But cannae we, as the people of the land, make suggestions or comment on what is transpiring? 'Tis our land, too."

He ran his hand through his dark locks, straightening them from the wind. "I would tend to agree with you, as would most philosophers, but unfortunately, many kings do not see things that way."

"And where is King Edward on these issues?"

He clapped his hands together and said, his eyes

sparkling, "That is the most important question every member of English and Scottish nobility should be asking, but few of them would dare. At present, his view is that he should rule both England and Scotland."

"And his method for ensuring it happens is to massacre my people. 'Tis a shame he cannae find a less violent way to see his wishes come to fruition. And what is yer belief, my lord?"

"I've told you all you need to know about my beliefs. What you must keep in mind is that men will always be at war. We are competitive and many of us are power hungry. These are the men who cause all the problems. Finding one who spares women and children is difficult."

He hated to tell her the truth of her situation, but he needed her to understand this was not a small turmoil that would end quickly. She needed to prepare herself for a long-term situation. Then he added, "Some believe that it takes a daft man to rule as a monarch."

"Or a daft woman? Do ye believe a woman can do what a man can?"

"I believe many women have the intelligence to rule, but it takes a certain callousness to do what is right. It also takes frequent and fast decision-making. Did you make the decisions for your family?"

She gave his question serious consideration. "I made small decisions, ones my husband was willing to entrust to me, such as what clothes to wash, what to cook, but the major decisions that affected us all, he made those alone. His last decision was not to go to the Highlands with his brother. He did not consult me on this decision, though I shared my opinion with him. I was told that this was a man's decision, not a woman's. Think you this man was wiser than this woman?"

Gabriel arched a brow to her, stunned that her husband had been so wrong. His family had left and he'd chosen to stay, condemning himself and the others to certain death, and his wife and children to kidnapping.

"As I said, some men are daft when making decisions." Deciding that continuing this discussion would not prove useful to either of them, he stood up and banked the fire, then said, "Why don't you relax for a bit, and I'll head down to the great hall to see what arrangements are made for those arriving to swear fealty to King Edward." Before he left, he added, "And I would advise you not to ask any of those questions in the hall where you could be overheard. It could be considered traitorous. Lock the door behind me and don't let anyone in until I return."

He left, adjusting his breeches and his leine shirt, not accustomed to dressing the way the tailor had outfitted him. The man had given him every piece of clothing that a Scottish laird would wear when around royalty.

Uncomfortable or not, he would play his part. From his perspective, things were looking up. They were well away from the Baron of Hepple, they'd likely be served fine food in the castle, and with any luck, Cara would be able to find out what many of the Scots thought of King Edward. He'd do his best to uncover whatever he could, as well.

He was about to step into the great hall when a woman stepped out of an alcove. "My, are you not a handsome one, my lord. Are you interested in a royal treat?"

She set her hand on her hip, her fancy red and silver gown sparkling in the light from the nearby torch.

He set his hand on the small of her back. "Mayhap another time, sweetling. I am expected inside." Then he winked and left. While he hated to play the part of the dandy, he knew in a castle this size, eyes were always watching. Interesting how quickly she'd come out of the alcove.

"Too bad, handsome," she said behind him. "Ye are a big one. I'd wager ye are everywhere."

He strode toward the hall again, but then took a quick turn in search of the kitchens. In a castle this size, he suspected there would be attached kitchens and separate ones, also. The number they fed was probably more than he'd ever seen at one sitting. He stepped outside to look for the external ones—which was when he ran straight into the very person he'd hoped to find, the cook of the castle. Harold was a big man, with a belly that spoke of his predilection for the food he made, but he had a heart of gold.

"Gabriel, I was not expecting to see you here," the man said, clapping him on the back. "'Tis been a long time since last we met. What brings ye this far north of the Borderlands?"

"Hush. I heard you were here. I came to advise you I've changed my identity. I go by the name Mac Henry and I have a wife with me."

"So soon after Della? Though I think 'tis a wise move for ye."

"It's a ruse, but I do like her, so please be kind to her. Don't ask many questions of me." He clasped the man's shoulder. They'd been good friends when he and Della had lived near the Borderlands, but everything had changed after King Edward had started his rampage. "So glad to see you, Harold."

"Spying?" Harold whispered.

"Our secret, my friend. Keep it close to you, if you please."

"My lips are sealed, but I must make haste to the back kitchens. If you need anything at all, send word to me there. I hope our paths cross again. Godspeed with ye."

He stepped away and headed back in through the front door, past the guards who had just seen him leave. Making his way through the maze of passageways, he explored as much as he dared, then made his way back to the great hall, surprised to see the number of different plaids inside.

There were many here to swear fealty. How many did so genuinely?

He grabbed an ale and sat at a table of three men. The others greeted him with nods, their demeanor friendly enough. "Greetings to ye. My wife and I have just arrived. What time is the meal and when will the fealty ceremony take place?"

One man said, "Food starts as soon as the sun

sets. This eve will be full of minstrels and merriment. Your fealty is to be sworn on the morrow."

Perfect. Cara would have to work her magic this eve.

How he prayed she could do it, though the thought of her rubbing her best features against another man made him wish to keep her inside their chamber. He'd much rather spend the entire night making love to her and teaching her about pleasure.

Instead, he'd be suffering from one of the sharpest invisible pains.

Jealousy.

⚘

Cara couldn't stop her body from trembling. One of the lavish gowns had arrived, a beautiful shade of dark blue with gold trim. She had never worn anything so elegant. Gabriel had arranged for a maid to come to her chamber to help with her hair, and it was lovely. She'd thanked the lass so many times that Gabriel had finally glared at her to stop.

He'd called her beautiful, and for the first time in her life, she *felt* beautiful. Now she just had to do what she'd been ordered to do, find as much information as possible about the many Scots here. The thought of doing so made her feel guilty and wrong—what would George think of her?—but her children's welfare was at stake. While he had cared more about making a stand than protecting their sons, she didn't feel the same way. She would do anything for her sons. Anything. How she hated not knowing who cared for them or how they fared.

With all of her ablutions done, she let Gabriel lead her into the great hall. They slowed as they entered the gathering space, and he leaned in to whisper in her ear, his warm breath sending shivers down her spine. "You are gorgeous this eve, lass."

She thanked him, but whispered back, "Hardly a lass."

"Ye'll always be my lassie," he said with a wink.

The great hall was full, revelers and Scots filling every corner, but the English had made a mark on the gathering. Plenty of English guards and knights stood sentry as a warning to the many Scots inside.

While they may be on Scottish land, in a Scottish castle, it was controlled by King Edward. How glad she was that he was not present. She'd be sorely tempted to bite *his* finger, like she'd done with the baron.

Since they stood alone, waiting for the food to be brought out and spread across the many tables, she whispered to him, "Do ye think 'twill work?"

"Aye. Do as I suggested. Once the meal is over, ye can leave as if to use the facilities, but do so slowly. Trust me when I say ye'll be followed. Flirt and brush. Ye'll get yer answers, but dinnae rush it. Allow them to lead the way. I'll always be watch-ing, so fear no' that 'twill go too far."

She ate little, her stomach too upset for the heavy fare. Lost as a wee bairn, her gaze continuously traveled the hall, wondering which Scot would dare to follow her.

"If ye keep staring at all the men, they'll no' think much of ye. 'Twould do ye better to rid yerself of the anxious look on yer face and pretend to enjoy yer husband," he said, wrapping his arm around her shoulder. "Allow me to feed ye, my sweet."

Turning to face him, she was struck by his confidence. By how strong and dashing he looked. His brown hair was freshly washed, curling just a touch at the ends, and seeing him in full Scottish regalia made her insides flutter. No man had ever affected her so. Mayhap she should feel guilty for harboring such a thought, but she couldn't forget the way George had endangered them. The way he'd wanted her and her sons to sacrifice themselves. Still. Why did the kindest man she'd ever met have to be an Englishman?

"Ye'll no' be able to choose him. He'll be chosen when he leaves the hall and ye follow. 'Tis that simple, though I have my eye on a few I think will be more fruitful for ye." He stuck his dagger in a piece of baked apple. "Try this, lassie. King Edward sent spices for the cook. This has cinnamon on it."

Her eyes widened as she touched her tongue to the warm apple. The taste was unlike anything she'd ever tried. Taking the bite he offered, she bit into the sweet delicacy and gave a small moan of delight.

Or she thought it was a small moan. Apparently it wasn't as quiet as she had thought because four men at the next table turned to stare at her, their mouths open.

She blushed and chewed on the treat, her eyes on Gabriel's. "They're staring."

"Dinnae despair. 'Tis exactly what I'd hoped, but more importantly... Ye like the cinnamon?"

"I've no' tried anything similar. 'Tis quite lovely," she whispered with a quick grin, indicating that she'd like another bite with a tip of her head.

"More, my pretty?" He waggled his dark eyebrows at her, spearing another bite of the apple with his knife. He held it for her and her tongue tested it first before she bit into it, hiding her moan of delight this time.

But they still stared.

He whispered, "Time for ye to go to the garderobe. I'll escort ye, but I'll hang back. Worry not. I'll always be watching."

She stood and he joined her, his hand at the small of her back. There weren't many wives in attendance, something she'd ask him about later. Just as Gabriel had said, many gazes followed her as she made her way to the passageway.

Gabriel was correct. Several of the men left their seats to follow.

The minstrels passed her as they entered the hall, preparing to entertain the many people who were feasting inside. She glanced in both directions, but Gabriel's solid hand at her back sent her in the direction of the garderobe. He stopped to speak with someone and motioned for her to move away on her own.

She did, her chin lifted and the sway of her hips a bit more pronounced than usual. She tended her needs, seeing no one, but as soon as she started back down the passageway, a man stepped out of an alcove to stand directly in front of her. "Greetings, my lady. Ye are a fine beauty. Yer name?"

"Cara, my lord. And ye are?"

"Seamus. Are ye married?"

"Aye, but my husband and I have a special arrangement." She and Gabriel had discussed some of the ways she could approach men and answer their questions.

Seamus gave her a sly grin and a wink, then leaned forward to whisper in her ear. "That pleases me."

She deliberately leaned toward him, brushing her breasts against him, although she doubted it would have the reaction Gabriel had promised.

But it did. She heard the man's intake of breath. To her surprise, he pulled her close and kissed her hard on the lips, something not the least bit exciting to her.

He ended the kiss abruptly and said, "Ye did no' open for me."

"We just met. How do I know if ye are true to our king or if ye plan to run into the forest?" Gabriel's suggestion came quickly to her. "I dinnae open for everyone." She gave him a sly look, waggling her eyebrows at him.

Seamus dropped his lips to her ear and said, "I hear many are heading to the Highland forests once they leave here. Are ye? If so, I'll find ye."

Fortunately, another man came their way, clearing his throat, so she stepped back quickly, dropping her hand from Seamus's forearm. While Seamus was flame-haired like her, this man was dark-haired, tall, and quite handsome. Seamus took off, casting a fleeting smile her way once he passed the new man.

"My lady, are ye in need of assistance?" the approaching man asked, his voice deep and smooth.

"Nay, I am fine. I must return to my husband." She started to pass him, but he gripped her elbow to stop her.

"Please, allow me to know yer name," he whispered. "'Tis no' often I can gaze upon a beauty such as ye. Yer red hair is intoxicating," he said, pausing to gaze into her eyes. "And ye have the green eyes of a true Scot, my lady."

His eyes were a silvery gray and seemed to reach down to her soul.

"Mine is Cara. Ye must tell me yer name. Who are ye?"

"My name is Grainger." He took a step closer, so close that she feared what he might do next. She was not prepared for this level of pretense. "Yer necklace is unique but quite lovely, even though the blue doesnae match yer eyes."

Who *was* this man?

CHAPTER SEVEN

GRAINGER SAID, "YE ARE THE loveliest lady here. Could we stroll a bit together?"

"Aye," she said. Her voice came out in a constricted tone because she simply didn't know what to make of this man. Of this situation.

He led her away from the direction where Gabriel was standing, deep in conversation with a man. Without alerting his companion to anything, Gabriel gave her a quick glance—a silent warning to be careful—and casually answered a question. How she wished she had his composure. The stranger's body felt strong against hers, and it brushed her in intimate ways that confused her. George would never have brushed against her where others could see.

"Why are ye here?" he asked.

"To swear fealty to King Edward, of course. Are ye here for a different reason?"

"I came for the same reason, but I am more interested in ye. Tell me, how loyal are ye to King Edward? Are ye a true Scot?"

She had no idea how to answer that. In her heart

she was true, although not so much so as George. Her husband had been so devoted to the cause he'd attempted to sacrifice his entire family on its altar. She would protect her boys at all costs. Besides which, she now knew there were good Englishmen as well as cruel ones. And so she deflected the question. "I hear many are headed to the forests."

"Aye, along with our true leaders, Wallace and Bruce. Would ye be willing to help us?"

Stunned by his question, she struggled to form an answer. But in the end there was no need.

Gabriel came down the passageway. "There ye are, my sweet. I thought ye were lost."

Something flashed in Grainger's eyes, but he turned her around and stood next to her. "She was lost. I was doing my best to direct her back to the hall, but I am a wee bit lost myself. Grainger Keegan. And ye?"

"Gabriel Mac Henry. This is my wife, Cara. My thanks for watching over her."

Grainger nodded to her and took his leave, not saying another word.

"Did ye learn anything from him?" Gabriel asked as soon as he was out of hearing.

"Nay," she lied, afraid to say anything about Grainger. A strange sensation had come over her upon meeting him. Almost as if they'd met before. She didn't wish to mention their conversation because she wasn't quite sure how she felt about it

He'd wanted her to help Wallace and the Bruce. Part of her longed to do just that, but how could she help Scotland without harming her sons?

Not wanting to let on, she quickly changed the subject to the first man she'd met. "I met a man named Seamus, and he did just as ye said. I brushed against him, and before I knew it, he was telling me that a number of Scots here would be running to the forests of Scotland as soon as they left Edinburgh. He wanted to say more, but Grainger interrupted him."

"Good! Did he say he would be joining them?"

"Aye, but he said little else because ye found us."

"Ye've had a great start. And they did no' misuse ye?"

"Nay," she said with a sigh. "They both touched too much for my comfort, but ye told me 'tis necessary."

"Aye. Ye are quiet. Are ye sure naught else happened?"

"Nothing. 'Tis all just so new to me. The royal castle, the food, the clothing. 'Tis a bit much. Must I stay down here for much longer?"

"Aye, we cannae disappear yet. Come back inside and we'll wander about, see who we meet."

She nodded, but her mind was with Bryan and Brice. What were they doing? Were they warm and well-fed? Although she knew he might not tell her, she could no longer refrain from asking. "If I do this, will I have my lads returned in a sennight? They are with someone ye trust?"

"Aye, they are safe. I've told ye they are well cared for. Do ye no' have any faith in me? Especially after I said children should not be victims of war? As for when ye may see them, I cannae make that decision. If ye wish to make the baron happy, ye must have something solid to give him. Ye must keep asking. If ye bring back news, I'm sure ye'll at least gain a visit with yer boys."

She couldn't help but be disappointed because she wanted this charade to be over.

She wanted her lads back.

※

Gabriel knew she was lying about Keegan, but he didn't know why. Why wouldn't she tell him what the man had said? He suspected it had to be one of two things. He'd either made such a crude suggestion that she was too embarrassed to repeat, or he'd propositioned her in some way.

But what way?

He set his hand on her back and led her back into the great hall, where the minstrels were playing their instruments and some couples were dancing. Most of the guests were wandering about and talking. One scan of the hall told him the conversations likely weren't of the sort they wished to overhear. People wouldn't talk privately amidst so many watching eyes.

He didn't doubt that many of these Scots were not truly loyal to King Edward, vows aside. He guessed at least half of them were here because they feared retribution against their clans or their closest kin.

He didn't doubt they had good reason to be afraid. War was an ugly mark on all who took part in it.

"Shall we walk and eavesdrop?" he whispered to his companion. Although he doubted they'd hear anything of value, perhaps they'd at least glean a better idea of who was present.

She nodded but he noticed her gaze had locked on Grainger across the hall. The man was staring at her, his gray eyes beseeching. What had he said to her? Gabriel could see how drawn she was to him, but why? Perhaps he'd have to have a word in private with the man on the morrow. He feared Grainger Keegan had too much interest in her.

Aye, he was jealous and knew it, but it was also his job to keep her safe.

They moved from group to group, stopping occasionally, but the conversations they overheard snatches of seemed light and inconsequential. When they finally reached Grainger's area at the back of the room, Gabriel struck up a conversation with the man's companion, hoping Cara would speak with the gray-eyed Scot again. He had to listen to him, get a sense of what they'd spoken about earlier.

Grainger took the opportunity to lean over and whisper in her ear. "Run away to the Highlands with me." Gabriel heard clearly. "Away from the king. Away from the battles."

Raw fury filled Gabriel. He wanted to grab the bastard by the throat and throttle him. Or maybe stab him, cut off his bollocks. Who did he think he was to make such a proposition to a woman he thought to be Gabriel's wife?

Directly in front of him?

He ended his conversation with the other man and turned to look at Grainger. He was a bit taller than the Scot, but other than that they were well-matched. "She'll not be going anywhere with ye," he said, leaving no doubt he'd heard every word. And he placed his hand on the hilt of his sword to underlay his message.

Grainger did the same. "Mayhap she feels differently."

Although part of him wished to challenge the arrogant man right there in the hall, they weren't here to draw attention to themselves. And so he turned to Cara and said, "Come, love. I tire of the company here."

She put her hand in his and followed him out of the hall, but not without one final glance over her shoulder.

Once they were back inside their chamber, he couldn't help himself. "Are ye out of yer mind? Ye let him think ye would leave with him?" He paced the room while she stood next to the hearth, tugging at the ribbons and ties on the back of her gown in a way that reminded him she wasn't used to such finery.

He stopped in front of her and said, "Turn around. I'll undo yer ribbons. I do hope ye remember what is at stake here."

"I understand," she finally said. Quiet descended on them as he carefully undid the ribbons, his fingers occasionally brushing across the soft skin of her back, from the top down to the tempting curve at the bottom, a place where his lips belonged, where his hands could reach down to caress her backside.

He ran his hand down his well-trimmed beard, doing his best to tame the wild urges in his traitorous body. In fact, he wished his beard was down to his chest so he could tug on it even more, but he kept it short. He'd need something to calm his need for this woman and his jealousy. The longer he was with her, the harder it was to fight the urges. When he'd finished unlacing the gown, she spun around and glared at him, pushing at his chest. "Ye think I'm no' aware of what's at stake, that my lads arenae with me? I think on it every moment of the day. Ye sent me into a new world and told me to flirt. I did. How was I to prevent the men from making a proposal? That man would have told me more about the Highlands if ye'd let him. He wasnae doing anything inappropriate. Howbeit, if he were, please tell me what I should have done to stop him, because I dinnae know how to stop a man stronger than me from doing as he wishes. I just want to finish this and return to my boys. To hell with all of ye."

She left him, stepping behind the partition to remove her clothing.

Gabriel felt like a bastard.

He couldn't argue with anything she'd said. She was in a new situation with a strange man, and she was by far the most beautiful woman in the hall. Two hundred men and a handful of women, and she was easily the prettiest.

What had he thought would happen?

He cursed himself as he heard her fall into bed, swearing he'd apologize on the morrow. Hell, but he hated this assignment, too.

Because the truth was that the jealousy of seeing her with another man was more than he could handle.

※

The fealty swearing was the quietest gathering Cara had ever seen. She had a difficult time reciting the necessary words, but she reminded herself that her lads' lives depended on her taking this oath, false or not. Forced or not.

Most of the people who'd gathered at Edinburgh probably felt the same way, though she noticed Grainger Keegan's words came out loud and strong, something she had not expected. He stood far behind them, but his voice echoed across the chamber filled with attendees. She and Gabriel were both quieter and more subdued. They did as they were asked without any celebration, standing as far off to the side as possible. The meal that night was a solemn affair.

Some headed home the following day, but many remained due to promises of a boar and venison meal that eve with more musicians and minstrels for entertainment.

"This eve will be verra important for both of us," Gabriel told her as the strolled outside through the gardens. "Ye must seek out the ones most likely to reveal secrets. I'll help ye determine which are best." There were others around, and so he stayed in his brogue and Scottish attire.

"Please do. I know no' who will reveal secrets without accosting me at the same time," she whispered. Men like Grainger unsettled her. They acted as though they cared for her, yet they didn't truly know her. She wasn't sure how to react.

"Ye must be careful, but rest assured I'll always be nearby." Gabriel stopped to speak with a man she did not know. The smile he gave the man was genuine and full of warmth, so it did not surprise her when he said, "This is Harold. He has been a friend for many years. Harold, stay with her a moment, if ye dinnae mind."

When he nodded, Gabriel turned and headed back inside.

Harold moved closer. "My lady, ye are a lovely lass. Please be careful. I've heard rumblings about a beautiful woman here, and I'm guessing they refer to ye. Remember that many of the people ye'll meet here are not what they seem."

She wasn't sure what to make of this large man with the large belly, but he had kind eyes. "What do ye mean by that?"

"This castle is controlled by the English, but no' long ago, it was controlled by the Scots. The English are all pleased by this, but no' all the Scots. Beware whatever a Scot tells ye. They may be loyal to their land or to the king. And many will no' dare tell ye the truth."

She thought about this comment for a few moments, realizing his words were true.

Which was Grainger?

When Gabriel returned, he thanked Harold and then ushered her back into the castle, his hand at the small of her back. "We have a delivery."

Her second lavish gown had arrived at the castle, a golden brown with ribbons that matched her hair. She preferred the blue, but this one was lovely also, with gold buttons across the bodice. Before the feast, the maid arrived to prepare her hair, weaving the golden ribbons through the design.

When Gabriel saw the effect, he couldn't stop staring at her.

"I gather this will work, my lord?" she asked with a smirk after the maid left.

"Aye, ye'll be turning many heads this eve, my lady." He smiled, but then pursed his lips. "Which also means ye must be careful. More careful than ye were the other night."

They headed toward the great hall. Many guests were wandering about, but they kept to themselves, observing the others as best they could.

"I think the more they whisper, the more likely they are to be true Scots. Do ye agree with me?" she asked in an undertone.

"I think ye may be correct." He leaned over to whisper his answer, his warm breath sending a sudden chill down her spine.

A small part of her wished that their odd relationship were true—that they were indeed husband and wife—but each time she felt tempted by this handsome and confusing man, she reminded herself that he was English. While he wasn't the one who'd killed her husband or any of their people, he had been traveling with the responsible group. Willingly.

So much had happened that her mind was dizzy with contradictory thoughts, but love or hate was often prominent.

When the meal started, they ate quietly, mostly because Cara was so focused on Gabriel. The warmth in his gaze, the tender touch of his hand at her lower back, the warm smile he was always quick to bestow on her—all of it mesmerized her more than the attentions of any of the other men, even Grainger. She couldn't help but wonder what it would be like to be married to a man who was so caring and handsome. One who was interested in her ideas and her mind. One who asked for *her* opinions.

Once the meal was finished, the musicians made their way inside and the guests began to get up and move about. Gabriel gave her the nod that it was time for them to seek information where they could, so they headed down the passageway that led to an open area where many of the guests had gathered to chat. It did give one the feel of being more private, but Cara knew better.

Nothing was safe in Edinburgh Castle.

They were stopped on their way to the door by a Scot wearing a green plaid, his hand grabbing Gabriel's arm. "Who are ye? I dinnae recall seeing ye at the fealty. Who is yer king?"

"We stood off to the side, but we were there," Gabriel barked. "Remove yer hand from my arm." He gave him such a fierce glare that the man dropped his hand.

"I'll remember ye, think on that," he said with a growl as he walked away.

"Do ye know him?" she asked.

Gabriel shook his head. "Move away from him. I dinnae wish to draw any attention. The men are suspicious of everyone. 'Tis the same as finding out your neighbor is ready to turn you over for hanging."

She scurried ahead of him, making her way through the crowd. As she did so, her gaze found a familiar face on someone at the edge of the group. Grainger.

She paused for a moment, but then moved forward. Gabriel leaned in to whisper, "I dinnae like that one, nor do I trust him. Be verra careful. Some Scots are conniving manipulators."

It was on the tip of her tongue to remind him that *she* was a Scot, and that most Englishmen in her acquaintance were cruel and power hungry, but it wasn't the time. They stopped to talk to a few men along the way, but everyone was tight-lipped about anything other than the feast. A short time later, a man waved to Gabriel from just beyond a side door. It was the same man they'd met earlier. Harold was motioning for them to follow him, so Gabriel took her elbow and headed out the door, following the big man into the cool night air. Something made her trust Gabriel's friend implicitly, although she didn't understand why. Mayhap it was his kind look.

Once they were alone, Harold said, "I've heard

something." His gaze searched their immediate area before he continued, "About where the Scots are meeting."

"Where?"

"Stirling."

"The castle?" Gabriel asked, still speaking in a low tone so as not to be overheard.

"Nay, the forests around Stirling." He pulled Gabriel away from her, making it clear he did not wish to be overheard, so she didn't attempt to follow. She glanced around instead, surprised to see other groups of men whispering furiously. So they weren't the only ones looking for information about the Scots' plan. She couldn't help but wonder what the man was telling Gabriel. Would he share the information with her?

She jumped when someone leaned over her shoulder from behind and whispered, "Will we see ye in Stirling?"

She spun around, not surprised to see Grainger standing behind her. He grinned and walked away, waggling his brow at her. What did all of the whispering and secretive plans mean exactly? Harold's words from earlier were proving to be truer than she'd guessed.

It was impossible to tell where anyone's loyalty lay.

Part of her didn't wish to know. Although she needed to save her lads, she loathed the thought of helping the English against her own countrymen. What if the information she passed along caused deaths?

Perhaps she could tell the baron only a partial truth.

Or maybe she could plant a seed of misinformation in the baron's mind? Something that would lead the English to do the wrong thing?

Nay. If it were only her, she would do exactly that—lie. Say something to sabotage the English, but she couldn't do it if it put her lads at risk.

Never.

Gabriel clasped the man's shoulder and said, "Many thanks, my friend."

The man hurried toward the castle, and once he was out of hearing, she asked, "Who is Harold? How do ye know him?"

"He's the cook here," Gabriel said. "As I said, I've known him for many years. I wonder if what he heard is true? 'Tis important information, if so. I want ye to start moving about and ask questions. Bring up Stirling Castle, how lovely it is. See if anyone seems particularly interested in discussing Stirling." He led her back inside through the side door, and she was surprised to see that the groups had scattered already. That made their departure quite obvious. Would anyone take notice? "We've both heard talk of the Scots gathering in the forests around Stirling, but Harold has heard talk of the castle. Which is it?"

All of a sudden, Gabriel tugged her out of the main walkway into an alcove. "Be quiet and kiss me. The guards are watching us."

With no time to react, she succumbed to his request as his lips melded with hers, his tongue pressing against her lips until she parted them, allowing him into a place only her husband had been before.

But her husband had never kissed her like this, and she knew not how to react. So she stopped thinking and gave herself over to feeling instead, tentatively touching her tongue to his. He made an odd sound and hugged her tightly to him, bringing her so close she could feel his muscles, his heat, his throbbing member pressed against her belly.

A new sense of power came over her, as she realized she was in possession of a skill she'd never dreamed of having—the power to entice a man. She arched against him, her hands snaking around his neck, playing with his long strands of hair until they both were panting. He responded eagerly, his hands moving around to clutch her bottom, the sensation of his hands on her flesh so powerful her knees nearly buckled.

He ended the kiss abruptly and she gripped his upper arms, afraid to let go and crumple to the ground in a heap.

She'd never been kissed like that, nor had she ever enjoyed a kiss like that.

He gave her a small hug and whispered, "Forgive me, but the man who questioned us earlier must have sent guards to check on us. I dinnae wish to speak with them. We're meant to avoid notice."

She nodded, her cheeks a bright pink color, she was sure of it. "I dinnae mind at all. Are they gone?"

Checking the area, he said, "Aye." Then he grinned, kissed her forehead, and whispered in her ear, "Nor did I mind it. Ye are a passionate one, lass."

They stepped back into the passageway, mostly empty but for a few men and couples mingling about, whispering to each other. Someone shouted a greeting to Gabriel, and he turned his head. Cara recognized the man who'd called to him as his friend, the cook. "I'll return quickly," Gabriel said. "Dinnae move."

He hurried over to the cook's side, his back to her—and a moment later, a hand snaked around her middle from behind, pulling her in the opposite direction. She nearly screamed, but a familiar voice said, "'Tis only me."

Grainger turned her to face him. "I dinnae like your husband, nor do I trust him. Ye dinnae act like husband and wife. Is he holding ye against yer will? If so, I'll save ye from him."

She shook her head. A sudden panic overtook her that someone could remove her from the only man who had ever truly protected her. She did not wish to be separated from Gabriel. There was something between them that she didn't understand.

"I hear there will be a gathering near Stirling Castle, that the English will meet the Scots there for battle," Grainger said. "*He* will take ye there. I'll take ye to safety. Ye shouldnae be involved. Ye're just a lady. Ladies dinnae belong in the war."

Gabriel's voice carried to her. "Take yer hands from her."

Grainger let go of her and rushed back inside the

great hall without another word. He clearly did not wish to deal with Gabriel directly, nor could she blame him. His voice had been full of hot rage.

She was grateful when Gabriel returned to her side. Grainger's intensity had frightened her. She'd worried he'd pull her away without her consent.

"What did he want?" he asked.

"He confirmed what yer friend said about Stirling. Grainger said I dinnae belong in the war. I think he suspects we are no' truly husband and wife."

She quickly chastised herself for having said anything at all.

Had she just given an important secret away to the English?

CHAPTER EIGHT

W HEN THE SENNIGHT WAS UP, they returned to Bothwell Castle with the information about the gathering at Stirling. Although she felt guilty for working against her countrymen, she needed to protect her sons.

Not much had changed in their absence, but the stable lads informed them that there were many more men in chains in the prison tower for suspected treason.

Cara had never felt so exhausted in all her life.

Gabriel helped her down from her horse, but he wasn't quick to remove his hand from her arm. "Lass, ye have dark circles under yer eyes. Why did ye not ask to ride with me? You could have leaned against me and slept."

Cara said, "Ye need no' use yer brogue, Gabriel. Yer back in with the English. There's no need to pretend any longer."

It hurt to hear him talk like one of her people, to be truthful. It made it more difficult to remember why she shouldn't trust him. Why she shouldn't have feelings for him.

"You are correct, but you evaded my question. Didn't you sleep last eve?"

"Nay," she said, deciding to tell him the truth. "I long to see my lads. I fear something may have happened to them. I've had dreams…"

"Hopefully, the baron will be pleased enough with your information to allow you one trip to see them." He held the door for her, and they stepped into the hall on the first floor of the tower. "Come, I'll take you abovestairs to clean up. Then we'll return to speak with the baron."

"Please do not make me wait too long. I must know about my sons," she pleaded. She'd never been away from them for so long. This separation was extremely painful for her, especially since she knew the boys were frightened and grief-stricken over the loss of their father, but she didn't know how to make them understand. They were men, and men who lacked children.

"I'll see what I can do. In the meantime, I'll send a bath up for you. Find a clean gown, one you had before. Save the lavish ones in case we must return to Edinburgh Castle."

She climbed up the stairs, level after level, her legs so tired she thought she might fall back down and land in a heap at the base.

Would she care?

Aye, the lads needed her.

Once inside, she settled what few belongings she had before the tub was brought into her private chamber. She'd forgotten to take her saddlebag off her horse, so she didn't have much. Gabriel paced in the other chamber, his presence a comfort. It made her feel safe to know he was there, watching the door. Keeping the baron away. She took a linen square to wash the dirt and grime of the road from her face, sighing with pleasure when she finally immersed her tired bones in the warm water. Ducking her head under the water, she proceeded to wash away all the smells of Edinburgh.

She had nearly fallen asleep in the warm water when a knock landed on her door. "I'm busy. Please come back."

Gabriel's voice carried through to her. "Ready yourself for the baron. He will be here in a quarter hour. I must report to the steward. I'll return as soon as I'm able. Just be truthful with him."

"I'll do my best," she said, climbing out of the tub and drying herself off, ignoring the way her legs trembled beneath her. This was what she'd been waiting for. She'd done as he asked, she'd learned potentially useful information, and once she shared it, she would be allowed to see her lads.

While she dressed, she closed her eyes to envision their beautiful faces. Brice still had just a wee bit of bairn about him, but Bryan would be showing signs of manhood before long. She only hoped he'd cooperate with his captors. She'd seen that brave look on his face as he stood beside his sire, prepared to make a stand. Oh, thank goodness he'd known to run and hide in the end.

Donning her gown, she did her best to smooth the wrinkles, then plaited her hair even though it was still damp. She put her boots back on and stepped into the other chamber, pleased to see the baron had not yet arrived.

She didn't have to wait for long.

The baron burst into the room without knocking. She stood, but then quickly sat down again. Two of his men were with him. At least they would not be alone together.

"Where is Gabriel?" she asked, expecting to see him behind the group.

"He'll return shortly, but we need not wait for him. Tell me what you've learned."

She nodded and gathered her thoughts before she spoke, folding her hands in her lap. "My lord, different men spoke of a small group of the attendees who would take the oath and then make their way into the Highlands. They suspected some would hide in the forests in order to join forces with Bruce and Wallace."

"Names. Who will be going into the forest?"

Names? She hadn't given that a thought. She only knew two. Seamus, no last name, and Grainger Keegan. Despite having felt unsettled by her last encounter with Grainger, she hesitated to give his name. She only hoped Gabriel wouldn't do it for her.

"They never informed me of any names," she lied. "'Twas a general statement about a group of Scots who would not honor their vow."

His fist pounded on the table. "I want names. Where exactly are they headed? Perthshire? Glencoe? Stirling? Ayr? I need specifics."

"No one told me any specifics." She hadn't

intended to lie about this. It wouldn't do her any good unless Gabriel backed her up, for he knew the true answer. And although she wished to think Gabriel would lie to protect her, he was an Englishman. But she couldn't tell the baron. She simply couldn't bring herself to do it.

"What good is the information if you don't know who or where? Do you have any idea how large the Highlands are or how easily a man could get lost there? Are you good for anything at all?"

"I'm sorry," she boldly lied, "but I dinnae have that information. They never told me."

He came around the table and grabbed her by the arm, lifting her off the chair, holding her so close to him that his spittle landed on her cheek. "Where? Where, I said?"

"If I knew, I would tell ye."

He threw her back into the chair, then paced a circle around the small table. "You'll go back, and you'll find out who and where. You will leave on the morrow. Understood?"

"But what about my sons? Ye said I could visit them after I returned. I want to see my lads." She stood up and placed her hands on the table. He had to give her this one boon. He'd promised. Even if he wasn't happy with her information, she'd learned something. And perhaps Gabriel could tell him about Stirling without revealing she'd known, too. "Please, just for a wee bit."

"You will not see the boys until you find out where the Scots are hiding." He stopped on the other side of the table, his hands on his hips, glaring at her.

"But ye promised," she said, a sudden fury lighting her insides.

"You'll see them in a fortnight. Go back and get the information I requested. You'll see your sons as soon as you return with it."

"A fortnight? 'Tis a long time." He ignored her and headed toward the door, acting as if she no longer existed, but she wasn't going to let him get away. The fear and horror in her sons' eyes wouldn't allow that. "Please. I must see them." She chased after him and stopped directly in front of him.

"And I denied you. Get ready to leave. You're nothing but a whore." His sentence came out in a sneer that matched the cruelty in his gaze.

She scrambled to come up with more information, something that would change his mind. She had to see her lads. "All right," she said, desperate. "I did hear something. Stirling. The Scots are meeting in the forests around Stirling."

He glared at her, his hands on his hips. She'd never seen such merciless eyes before. "You kept that from me. You will pay for it. You'll not see the lads for a moon. Perhaps I'll kill one of them so you'll learn to follow my instructions."

The threat to her lads undid her. She lost all control of her actions. Furious, she pushed the baron back against the door, hard enough that his head hit it, and shouted at him, "Dinnae touch my lads!" One of his men caught him and righted him.

His gaze narrowed and he said, "Five lashes for her. Do it near the stables so all can watch. You never touch me. Never!" he cried, pointing his finger into her face. "Get her ready and find me the whip."

Startled, she mumbled, "Whip? Lashes? What? I just wish to see my sons. Ye took them from me!"

The knight closest to her grabbed one of her arms and dragged her out the door. She wanted to kick and spit and scream, but she refused to beg. The bastard had used her and lied. She may have lied, too, but he'd put her an impossible position, pitted between her people and her family.

She wanted her lads.

They pulled her down the staircase roughly and she fought to stay upright. Once they were outside, one word traveled like wildfire through the knights. "Whipping." The word created a buzz through the men, and although a few looked disgusted, many of them seemed excited, as if the sight of a woman's lashing would be pleasant. Several men even hurried to reach the stables before it started.

They were all daft.

One of the baron's men pulled her over to a post outside the stable, treating her as carelessly as if she were cattle. He tied her arms to the post above her head and tore the back of her dress open while the other went inside. "I'll get the whip."

Still stunned at what was happening, her entire body reacting with a mix of fear and fury, she never said a word until the first crack of the whip and the resulting sting seared her skin. It burned unlike anything she'd ever experienced before. She refused to call out to give the bastard the satisfaction of hearing her cry or scream.

But by the third lash, the scream she heard was her own.

She wished to die.

꽃

Gabriel struggled with all the information he had. Harold had informed him of the large number of English on their way to Stirling Castle, but he wasn't sure what to do with the information. He'd have to bide his time if he wished to accomplish his original goal of exacting vengeance on Della's killer, but every day his tolerance was sorely tested.

He'd found a waterfall nearby after finishing with the steward and was busy washing up when the squire Wyot came flying toward him on horseback. "My lord, my lord, hurry!"

The boy's wild eyes alarmed him even more than his tone.

"What is it?" he asked, stepping out of the water. Not waiting for Wyot's response, he tugged his tunic back on, grabbed his sword, and mounted his horse.

"The lass was sentenced to five lashes by the baron himself. They're nearly ready to do it!"

Hellfire, what had her feisty mouth said this time? He should have stayed. Hepple had sent one of the knights to him when he was with Stoddard, saying he'd found her asleep and would meet with her on the morrow. The delay had given him the opportunity to bathe, or so he had thought. He should have checked himself.

Lying bastard.

He mounted his horse and followed Wyot, coming abreast of the lad. "What happened?"

"She pushed him when he refused her request to see her sons."

He let out a loud bellow, then said, "He'll kill her."

He'd never had such a strong urge to protect someone. Going over his options, he decided he only had one: he'd have to take her away for a while.

Or forever, if necessary. He racked his brain for a safe place to take her, then he knew.

"What will you do, my lord?" Wyot asked innocently. He saw the hope in the boy's gaze—he truly believed Gabriel could right this wrong.

"I'm taking her far away."

"May I go with you?" the boy asked at once, his eyes wide. "I hate the baron. He whips people whenever it pleases him, and he rations the food out as if he were the king. Why can he not be considerate of others?"

He glanced over at him and said, "You may, but only if you can ride quickly."

"I will, my lord. I can help you. Please let me help you!"

"Then stay right behind me. I'll not stop for you. I'll be carrying a woman in pain."

"I'll be there."

He came into the clearing in time to hear Cara erupt in a heart-wrenching scream. The look on the baron's face was one of satisfaction, of almost sensual pleasure, and it disgusted Gabriel so much that he didn't need to think twice. He rode his horse in, jumped off, and caught the baron by the side of his blade so hard that he knocked him out. While he wished to run the baron through with his sword, he knew he'd be hanging from the nearest tree by morn if he killed him, and what would happen to Cara and her boys?

Three men came at him with their weapons, but he took two out with one arc of his great sword, finishing the third with his backswing.

The baron was out cold and the others had run for their weapons, so he didn't hesitate. He cut Cara's wrists free and she crumpled into his arms. "I have you, but I cannot promise it won't hurt."

She lifted her head up and kissed his cheek. He set her on his horse rather clumsily, but she managed to stay mounted until he jumped up behind her, grabbing the reins of his horse and sending his stallion into a fast gallop.

As he raced away as fast as possible, he caught sight of a few horses out of the corner of his eye. Only they weren't saddled, and they were running as if being chased. He guessed that his friend had opened the door to the stables and put a fright in the horses. A few moments later, Wyot came chasing up behind him with a wide grin on his face, an extra horse behind him. The lad was quick-thinking.

Slowing just a bit to allow the lad time to catch up with him, he said, "We ride fast and hard. They'll follow us for a while, but they won't be able to keep up. Good move with the horses and saddling the extra horse to take with us."

"This sweet beast was already saddled. I thought we may have need for another eventually. I hoped the free ones would trample the baron. Why did you not kill him? You had the chance."

"I did, and perhaps I should have, but they would have come after us in full force if I'd killed him. I feared for the woman and her boys. Don't worry, he'll get his just due, but not when he has fifty knights at his disposal."

He didn't admit to the lad that he had a powerful reason to keep the man alive—one he could not yet share with anyone. Time would see him punished for his cruelty, but not yet.

Cara fell against him, but then moaned and sat up straight, clutching his arm to keep from falling.

"I'm sorry, sweetling, but until I know we're safe, I cannot stop."

She nodded and fell against his chest sideways, and he tucked her in as best he could.

He did his best to ignore the blood on her back. If he looked at it again, he'd be forced to go back and beat Hepple until he took his last breath.

CHAPTER NINE

"WHERE ARE YOU TAKING ME?" Cara whispered against his chest.

He slowed his horse and reached into his saddlebag and pulled out a plaid. "Here, sit up and I'll cushion your back a bit. It's clean. We have to keep riding hard until they slow their pursuit."

"Ye've stolen me away?" she asked in disbelief. "But is that no' traitorous?" Although she'd hoped Gabriel would side with her over the baron, she'd never imagined he'd do something so directly in opposition to the man.

"The baron will consider it so, but I don't care what he thinks." He stopped his horse, helping her lean forward a wee bit, then tucked the plaid between them before returning her to her previous position. "Your temper got the best of you."

"Aye," she said. "He said I couldn't see the lads for a fortnight if I didnae tell him exactly where the Scotsmen were planning to lie in wait for the English soldiers. I told him then, but he was angry that I'd kept it from him. He said he'd keep the lads from me for a moon. I have to see my sons. I was no' thinking when I pushed him."

"How many lashes?"

"He said five, but I know no' if he completed them."

"She took three before you saved her, my lord," Wyot said, catching up to him. "That's what someone said. They were counting. How cruel is that?"

He moved her forward again, his touch impossibly gentle, so he could look. "Wyot's right. It looks like you took three. I got there in time. I don't know if you would have survived all five. I must get you to safety. Somewhere we can clean those."

"Where are we going?" She'd asked before, but he hadn't answered.

"To a cave I know. My sister married a Scot, so I know a small area in the Highlands not far from Stirling Castle. It's called Dunblane. There's a couple of caves there and it's not far from water. Hepple will never travel that far into the Highlands, but we'll be close enough to learn what transpires at Stirling. We can hide until he gives up, and he will. He has too many other projects he's working on. We'll hide, hopefully long enough to heal your back, then move on from there. Wyot can stay with you while I scout the area."

"My sons. Will ye take me to them?" She pulled back to gaze at him. "Please?"

"I cannot take you now. Trust me when I say they are safe."

"But what if Hepple goes after them?" she asked, fear flooding her. "Would he hurt my bairns because of what I did?"

"He would, if he knew where they were, but I never told him where I left them. Close your eyes, we must hurry. We'll talk once I've found a place for us to hide."

She hated that she had to take his word for it, but she had no choice but to trust him. Besides, he was right—if Hepple didn't know where her lads were, then he wouldn't be able to hurt them. She also knew he was right about the baron. From gossip she'd overheard, the man had sent out his knights and the others to destroy any small villages nearby. And now he would likely be going to Stirling or back to Edinburgh.

The cruel bastard would not be happy until he was whipping all of Scotland.

It was nearly dark when they stopped. She had no idea how long they'd traveled, but it seemed like hours. After advising Wyot to follow him closely, Gabriel led the way down a deep ravine, around a craggy knoll, and finally into a hidden clearing behind a copse of thick pines and brush. The sounds of a babbling burn echoed along with the tittering of red squirrels rustling the leaves above. He stopped in front of a tall outcropping, dismounted, and said, "I'll be right back."

Her gaze followed his tall frame as he climbed a path at the back end of the clearing. He climbed onto a ledge and then promptly disappeared.

"That must be a cave," Wyot said. He turned to her, his eyes nearly glowing with excitement. "We'll be safe here. Even the horses will not be seen. I knew he'd know where to bring us!"

Gabriel came out of the cave, though he had to duck. His lack of speed indicated it was safe, and indeed, he told them he'd found no signs of danger. He came back over to the horse and put his hands around her waist, lifting her effortlessly. He set her down next to him, his hands still on her waist, and said to Wyot, "What did you bring with you?"

Wyot climbed down from his horse, lifting his chin with a bit of pride. "When I freed the other horses, I grabbed the healers' bag and any other bags I saw on the horses. Then I stole a bag of apples and other treats normally kept for the horses. I thought we might have use of them."

Although Cara had taken note of the many saddlebags on his horse, she hadn't stopped to think what was in them. He was a smart lad, much like Bryan. The two boys would get along…if they ever met. The thought pained her, and she felt another powerful wave of longing for her sons.

"Good mind," Gabriel said with a smile. "Can ye walk, lass?" His brown eyes were so full of concern that she said a quick prayer of thanks for his presence.

"I'll be fine." She glanced down at her gown, finally registering that it had been ruined so her back could be revealed to the bastard. Although she was glad nothing rested against it, she was quite indecent.

"Lad, have you any healer's salve in there?" Gabriel asked. "And hopefully some plaids. We need something decent to keep her warm."

Wyot nodded. "And some linen squares and

some potion."

She glanced at the impressive array of bags he now held. "Ye also have one of my bags there. I believe I had one gown folded inside."

Wyot held up another bag. "Aye, this one was from your horse. I was going to bring it to you later. And I have two pairs of breeches and tunics, too. I'm always at the ready, my lady. A person must be prepared in a time of war."

"You're a wise lad," Gabriel said, patting him on the back with his free hand. "Once I get you settled, Cara, I'll find something to clean your wounds and put the salve on it. Hopefully, it will keep you from getting the fever. But I would suggest you wear the tunic and breeches. You'll see no one else here, and it will be easier for us to change your bandages with a tunic. Besides, breeches are much warmer. 'Twill be chilly sleeping this eve."

They made their way up to the cave, each step hurting Cara's back, but she bit back a moan. Once inside, she found a rock to settle on deep inside the small cave. The area where they'd gathered was a good distance from the entrance, and a little to the side, so they were protected from much of the wind. The opening was small, but it offered enough light, and there was plenty of room for the three of them. They could stand tall inside, even Gabriel.

He washed and dressed her wound with a tenderness that humbled her. Any gentleness George had once possessed had long since been shriveled by bitterness. She took the tunic and breeches from Wyot, hoping they'd fit, and tried them on while the men stepped out of the cave. Surprised they fit her so well, she decided she might like wearing breeches more often. When they were ready to settle for the night, Gabriel said, "Wyot, sleep closer to the opening so you can listen for anything unusual. I'll sleep back here with Cara."

She gave him a surprised look, so he reached out and tucked a strand of loose hair behind her ear. "Sweetling, with your wounds, you'll never be able to sleep on the ground. Your back will be too painful and it's too cold for you to sleep on your belly. You must sleep on top of me. I suspect it's the only way you'll be able to rest."

She stared at her boots, her feet already chilling from the night air. "You mean my belly to your belly? 'Tis most improper since we're not married." She had trouble looking him in the eye since the idea embarrassed her so.

"Lass, it's the only way. I promise not to do anything forward. Feel the stone floor. It's like ice."

She bent over, but the motion sent pain shooting through her. Tears pricked her eyes, but she'd not be dissuaded so easily. She forced herself to finish the movement by bending her knees to touch the floor. "'Tis verra cold."

"I have two extra plaids. I'll sleep on one and cover you with one. I'll give Wyot the fur because he's closest to the opening. Agreed? You're fully dressed," he said, a small smile as he looked over her new outfit. "And it suits you."

She considered his offer for a moment. He was right. Her back hurt more than she could bear, and she'd never be able to sleep on it. Sleeping on her side on stone would also be difficult.

Wyot stepped forward and said, "My lord is a gentleman. He'll not do anything wrong to you. He's a kind and proper man."

She finally conceded, and they settled down to rest. Wyot arranged his furs near the opening, and Gabriel found a flat spot. He arranged the bedding then lay down on his back, gesturing for her to join him. "You must come to me, lass."

Her heart beat so quickly that it frightened her. She trusted Gabriel, but would he prove honorable all through the night? And what if she accidentally rolled off him?

As if hearing her thoughts, he said, "I'll not let you roll because I'll have both arms holding you close."

She nodded, but the moment she attempted to bend over, pain shot through her, forcing her to stop and rethink her position.

"To your knees first." He patted the spot next to his waist. "Right here and I'll help you the rest of the way."

She slowly followed his instructions, her knees touching his waist. Her eyes closed at how intimate they were, but the cold, hard surface of the stone convinced her to continue. He was right—she'd never sleep stomach-down on the cold rock.

"Lean down and straddle me. You have breeches on," he reminded her. "Then you can straighten and settle your head on my chest."

She did as he asked, awkwardly, and let out a

small moan when she finally met his heat. How did men stay so warm? She settled against him exactly as he'd suggested, but he groaned when she straddled him, forcing her to jerk her head up. "Have I hurt ye?"

"Nay, Cara. You are a beautiful woman. It was a manly response to you, but I'll not do it again. Forgive me. Rest your head, and try to go to sleep."

They'd only lain there for a few minutes when Gabriel whispered, "You're not sleeping."

Her head rested sideways against his chest, the warmth he gave so welcome. He'd helped her pull the tunic over her wounded back, and the plaid he'd covered her with was soft and warm.

"Are you uncomfortable?" he whispered. "Tell me what I can do to help. You need sleep, Cara."

"I miss my lads. I was just thinking about them." Oh, how she missed them. Their laughter, their vibrant curiosity, and Brice still carried the sweet aroma of youth. "You're sure Hepple doesn't know where they are?"

"I swear it. I hid them well because I don't trust him."

"But why? Why are you helping me at all? How could it be worth the risk?"

He sighed and set his hand under his head, staring up at the roof of the cave. "I meant what I said to you when we first met. I don't believe men's wars should involve women and children. I wasn't planning on rescuing you, it just happened. My…"

She waited to see if he would finish the sentence. Some deep part of her wished to know this man, to understand him.

"I lost my wife. She was pregnant with our child, so I lost them both together."

"Gabriel, I'm so sorry. How horrible."

They lay in silence for several minutes, and it surprised her when he moved his hand to the back of her neck, massaging her lightly. How she wished to ask for the boon she needed. "Gabriel?"

"I know of what you'll ask me, lass. We'll go as soon as I feel it's safe. But I have a question for you. Do you wish your lads to see you in your present condition? And would it be more difficult for you if I had to take you away from them again? I fear your presence could endanger them until we are rid of this fight." He hated to upset her, but she was still considered a captive of the English.

"But it could go on forever, could it not?"

He thought for a long moment, his hand still caressing the back of her neck, the gentle caress nearly lulling her to sleep. She'd never slept this close to a man. George would do what he wished when he wished. Sometimes he'd hold her for a moment afterward, but they always slept apart. This was something unique to her, and she had to admit, she liked it.

Gabriel said, "This war against King Edward could go on for many years, but it will slow in the winter. The English knights will not be able to survive the Highland winters, not without food. Wallace burned many fields in the Lowlands to prevent the English from using them. I believe it was a wise move on his part. Without food for thousands of warriors, they cannot continue the onslaught.

"But it is said the Scots are in hiding and will attack the English when they least expect it. Hepple seeks information about their strategy, and once he finds it, he'll no longer bother us. This could be the ambush that's been discussed."

"Do ye believe there'll be a large battle?" She hadn't considered all the ramifications of the presence of the English in the Lowlands. True, the baron's people had easily defeated their small village, but he couldn't kill all of the Scots, could he? The Highland warriors were infamous for their ferocity.

"It's the first of September. I believe there will be a fierce meeting of the two forces within the next moon. Wallace is furious after what the English did to Berwick and the Borderlands. He will retaliate if he has the numbers."

She took in this information, wondering what it meant for her boys. She wondered where her parents were, her sister, her husband's clan. How difficult it was to be separated from everything she knew. Everything she'd ever known. "My thanks to ye for yer honesty. And I will answer yer question. I do not want my lads to see me as I am now. I wish to appear as I always have to them, and I dinnae wish for them to see any more of this fight. They've seen enough bloodshed. But I know no' how I'll be able to stand being away from them." She lifted her head and stared at him. "How can I go on?"

He gazed into her eyes and said, "We are but two hours from them. What if I allowed you to see them from afar? Would that soothe you?"

She felt her face split into a wide grin. "Aye, 'tis all I ask. If I could just see them…know they were safe and well."

"All right. We must wait at least one more day to be sure we are not followed, then we'll travel north." He brought his hand up to cup her cheek. "Will that please you?"

"Aye." She was so happy that she lifted her head and leaned closer, giving him a quick kiss on the lips.

He looked surprised, but then he said, "Lass, that was a tease. If it's a kiss you want, I think we could do better. Agreed?"

That was exactly what she wanted from this man, this savior, this fierce warrior for women and children. She wanted to taste him and get closer to him, even with all the pain inside of her. She leaned down and he cupped her face, his lips touching hers gently at first, then he deepened the kiss, a low growl coming from him as he tugged her closer. She parted her lips and he slanted his head, angling his mouth just so to give him better access, their tongues finding each other in the cold dark night, teasing and tantalizing with the promise of more. This man invaded her senses like no other had ever done.

She'd never experienced a kiss like this before—one that was so genuine, so raw with passion yet full of promise. He ended the kiss and reached for her underneath her arms, pulling her closer so she could tuck her head under his chin. The hardness of his erection pressed against her belly, and she couldn't help but wonder what mating with him would be like if a simple kiss could send her reeling.

She hoped she'd find out.

And she didn't care that he was English. She *was* falling in love with him.

CHAPTER TEN

GABRIEL STOOD NEAR THE BURN the next morn, washing up as best he could. The cold water was something he needed because he'd been sorely tested last eve. Having Cara's glorious curves melded against him had been the fiercest test of strength he'd ever experienced. But he'd survived.

He'd savored being close with her, and each time they touched each other, he sensed the possibility of unbridled passion in her. He would wager that she was quite innocent when it came to the pleasures of the body—and he would like nothing better than to be her teacher.

A part of him felt guilty, as though his heart was being unfaithful to Della, but they'd discussed their wishes early in their marriage—they'd agreed to pursue happiness with another should one of them die early.

If Della were here, he would stay by her side forever.

But she was not.

Cara was a strong woman who would risk her life for her boys, and he had to admire that. He'd also like to repay Hepple for striking a woman. *This* woman.

The bastard.

Wyot came running out to him. "She's awake, my lord."

The boy had proven a godsend in more ways than one. He'd already left the camp and come back with useful information.

"Wyot, call me Gabriel, please. I told you that long before we found Hepple."

In a small way, Wyot had become the son he'd lost. If the lad hadn't ridden off with them after Cara's whipping, he'd have gone back for him. Their loyalty to each other was something he treasured.

The boy nodded excitedly. "She's awake, *Gabriel*," he said, and scampered back to the cave.

Gabriel shook his head to himself, smiling slightly at the boy's exuberance, as he finished his ablutions and put his tunic back on. When he stepped inside the cave, he found the sack of apples Wyot had taken from the stable and took two of them. He handed one to Cara and settled onto a rock next to her. "How do you fare, my lady?"

She accepted the apple with a nod of thanks, then bit into it. "I am famished this morn. I owe ye both many thanks." Wyot stood to the side wearing a wide grin, something he often did. He'd found a piece of dried meat to chew on.

"If it suits you, I'll tend your wound, then I'll take you on the two-hour ride to observe your sons."

Her face lit up. "Ye will? But did ye no' wish to wait one more day?"

"Nay, Wyot went out early this morn and found out Hepple and his men are traveling to Edinburgh to meet with some of the king's men. My guess is they've also heard about Stirling and are meeting to plan their attack, something I am glad to not be a part of. If they choose to try to thwart the Scots, their attack must be timed perfectly. That will take time. This would be a perfect time for us to go. But you must agree to my terms."

"I will."

"Don't you wish to know what they are before you agree?" From her quick response, he suspected she'd agree to anything to get this boon, something he could use, should he ever need to do so, but she hadn't proven difficult to handle yet. She just had that feisty temperament to always take into consideration.

"I trust ye will not make demands I cannae meet. What are they?"

"You are not to speak with your boys. I expect they'll be doing some chores outdoors. And we will spend no more than a quarter hour observing them. After that, we must leave."

He couldn't help but notice the tears she fought to contain, but she quietly agreed. Her body trembled while he dressed her wound, cleaning it and applying more of the salve that would help fight off the fever. He covered it with fresh linens and padded the inside of her tunic with one of the plaids. "One of the three stripes on your back has nearly healed. The other two are still open, one worse than the other. Are you sure you'll be able to ride a horse?"

"Aye. I promise. Please, may we no' go now?"

"Wyot, bring a few apples, but leave the rest here. We'll return later, but we may make a stop at a nearby inn on the way back."

Perhaps seeing her sons would be a stronger salve than any healer could create.

※

The journey seemed interminably long to Cara. She made a point of memorizing all the landmarks they passed, and as they got closer, she could sense the lads were near. Finally, they arrived at the small manor home hidden in the pines. Gabriel pointed to a clearing a distance away from the home and dismounted there. "Wyot, you're to watch the horses and wait here. We shall return in less than a quarter hour. If you see anyone, please whistle."

Wyot nodded, and Gabriel helped her down, staying her with his hand. "Allow me to check first. Then I promise to return for you."

She accepted his dictate, rocking on her heels while she waited, but she trusted this man. He'd gone out of his way to protect her and her bairns, risking himself to do so.

Her feelings for him confused her to no end. Whether he was loyal to the baron or not, there was no denying he had been part of the group that had killed her husband. She had no idea if the others lived, but the English were killing her people.

How could she develop such deep feelings for one of them?

Or were her feelings shallower than she thought?

He returned and she fought the urge to run to him. When he got close, he held his hand out to her and said, "Promise me, not a word."

She put her hand in his and nodded her agreement, afraid that if she spoke to him now it would end their agreement. They meandered through the pines, moving soundlessly on the soft ground, until they came to the edge of the land behind the home.

He knelt behind a tree and tugged her down next to him, still holding her hand. Peeking through the sweet-smelling pine branches, she saw some chickens running about, cackling at each other. And then she saw them. Two lads moving about the clearing.

Her sons. She closed her eyes for a second, then looked again, afraid her mind had conjured them, but they were still there. Holding her breath, she did her best to overhear their conversation.

"But when will Mama be back?" Brice asked, looking up at his older brother, who was busy chopping wood.

"I dinnae know, but we must remain strong. She'll come for us soon. 'Tis what Hestra has told ye over and over again." He swung the axe over his head and split another log in two, then swung again to cut the larger pieces into smaller ones. "Stack them in a new pile, next to the tall one. We'll need all this wood for warmth."

The two continued working for a time, until

Brice said, "I miss Mama, do ye no'?"

Bryan finished his forward swing and leaned against the axe, picking up a water skin and taking a drink. Cara couldn't believe how much his upper body size had increased in such a short time. He was growing so quickly. He sweat and heaved just like his sire used to when cutting wood. He took another swig and said, "Of course I miss her. I miss Papa, too, but we'll no' see him again."

"But ye believe we'll see Mama again?"

"Aye. Ye will. And if we dinnae, always remember we have each other." Bryan returned to swinging his axe.

Cara covered her mouth to keep from crying out over her son's last comment. She squeezed Gabriel's hand and shook her head. She had to leave. It was too difficult to watch them and not reveal her presence.

She hurried back to the horses as soon as the crack of the axe covered the sound of their steps, pinching her eyes together in an attempt to stop the tears. She could not lose control or Gabriel would never bring her back to see the boys again.

Painful though it had been, her soul would rest easier knowing the lads were whole and together. This quick visit would sustain her for a while.

Once she made it back to the animals, Wyot whispered, "You saw them? They are hale?"

Still afraid to make a sound, she nodded to Wyot with a big smile, swiping at a couple of tears streaking down her cheeks. Seeing her lads was exactly what she'd needed to stay strong through the challenges ahead.

She knew this situation between the English and the Scottish was not going to end soon. And despite what Gabriel had said, she doubted the baron would ever forgive them for what they'd done. He lifted her up on his horse, a small act of kindness that pleased her, for she feared that she would probably collapse if she attempted it on her own. Her back hurt as though a horned owl had dragged its talons down her flesh over and over again, and her heart ached for her sons.

She'd vowed to stay strong for her boys and she had. Now she wished to sleep.

About an hour into their return trip, Gabriel said, "I'm going to stop. We are in Scotland, and I don't think the English are around. I'll adopt my brogue again and you are to treat me as a Scotsman. We'll hopefully get a bit of stew and see what we can learn. Agreed?"

"Aye. Warm food would be appreciated."

"And we'll get a couple of loaves of bread to take with us. We must be able to sustain ourselves in the cave. Wyot, do you have the gown for the lady I asked you to bring along?"

"Aye," the lad said. "Here in my saddlebag."

They stopped near an isolated inn on the main path. Gabriel had found a copse of trees where they could change their clothing. She managed to get her gown on and he loosely tied the ribbons in the back, encouraging her to wear her mantle to cover her injury. Once they were ready, they tied their horses near a grassy knoll and headed toward the inn.

"Please dinnae slip. I'm a Scot, as ye know." She couldn't help but smile at that, and when he looked at her, he smiled back. Gabriel's true smiles showed in his eyes. It struck her that he was trusting her, just as she'd trusted him. If she were to reveal him before a roomful of Scots, he would pay the price. Which meant he trusted her.

She found she quite liked that.

Before they entered the inn, Gabriel said, "Allow me to step in first to see if there is room for us."

Wyot stood at her side, and even though he was just a lad, she found his presence comforting. "My lady, dinnae worry about my lord. He'll be loyal to ye."

"Wyot, ye have a fine brogue, too. Where did ye learn it?"

"From Gabriel, of course. He's the best at everything. Do I sound the same?"

"Aye, ye do," she said. "Ye sound just like my eldest son."

"My thanks," he said, squaring his shoulders. "'Tis a fine compliment, I believe."

If he thought so, then she didn't much mind that she liked him. English and all.

A few moments later, Gabriel returned and said, "We can dine with the others, and ye'll no' be the only woman inside, a fear I had."

The din in the dining room hushed temporarily when they stepped inside, but the conversations had started up again by the time they were seated. The voices were loud, the sentiments bitter and predominantly against the English. If Gabriel wanted to learn what was happening, he'd chosen a good place.

Three bowls of aromatic mutton stew were served to them, along with three ales and a loaf of warm bread. All three ate heartily, but about half-way through their meal, Gabriel stood up and said, "I'm going to get another ale, see what I can over-hear on the way. Wyot, stay here with the lady."

She glanced around the room as she chewed on a piece of bread. There were at least ten tables with four to six stools around each one. The walls were decorated with every kind of weapon possible, swords and daggers everywhere. She had to won-der if it had been an intentional choice to ensure each person in the inn had a weapon should they need to use it.

She peered at some of the travelers, none of whom she recognized. Two women were with their husbands and they listened quietly to all the talk of the English and how they'd hurt the Scots.

How did Wyot and Gabriel feel about their con-versations since they sided with the English?

Her gaze carried to the last table and fell on a familiar face. It was Grainger, and his gaze was already locked on her. He smiled and made his way toward them, taking the seat Gabriel had vacated. She'd forgotten what a good-looking man he was.

Always thinking, he said to Wyot, "Fetch me another ale, if ye please?"

Accustomed to doing as he was bid, Wyot jumped up to get it.

She needn't ask why he'd been sent away. Grainger dropped his voice and said, "Cara, fate has brought us together. Leave with me today. Ye can help me. Please."

He reached for her hand, but she set it on her lap. Although Grainger was handsome, and she suspected she could find her lads again without Gabriel's help, she would not forsake him. Her heart no longer cared that he was an Englishman. There was so much more to him than that.

"I'm sorry, Grainger. Your cause is laudable, but I cannae help ye."

He gave her a hard look, his lips pinched into a straight line. "Think on it. I'm sure we'll meet again, and mayhap then ye'll remember which side yer on."

"I'm Scottish, Grainger, like ye. 'Tis the right side to be on."

"Is it?" he asked, getting up from his stool and leaving abruptly.

She watched him leave, wondering what his last message meant. If she had learned anything about Grainger through their interactions, it was that he appeared uncertain about his own beliefs. Sometimes, he wished to ferret her away from trouble, sometimes to dive into it. Sometimes he wished to declare himself Scottish, and sometimes English. He'd sworn fealty to the English, but was he one of the ones who had lied about it? She didn't know whether she could trust this man.

She glanced over at Gabriel. Even though he was English, she knew she could trust him when it came to the important things in life. If she were ever in trouble, he would help her. Would Grainger? Or would he change his mind again?

Something had shifted between her and Gabriel, something powerful.

She'd never leave Gabriel.

CHAPTER ELEVEN

TWO DAYS HAD PASSED WITH no new changes on the horizon. There'd been no mention of a battle at Stirling and no evidence of men moving about quickly. The sun hadn't come up yet, but she woke up shivering, forgetting she was in a cave and not in a soft bed in Edinburgh Castle. She sat up, searching for Gabriel, but he was nowhere to be seen. His warmth was no longer beneath her.

Deciding he must have gone out to relieve himself, she clustered the wool plaids together and lay on top of them, hating the cold of the stone. True, they'd been safe here, and they stayed dry, but she would be grateful to leave.

Except…where would they go?

That very question had kept her up in the night. She had no idea where her husband's clan had gone, or if any of the women and children from their small village had survived. If they had, they would have moved on and she had no idea where.

A woman with two lads to protect would have trouble making her own way in Scotland or

England.

Wyot stirred, so she spoke up. "Wyot, where's Gabriel?"

He rolled over and said, "He took an early ride to find out what was happening. He stopped at the inn and found out the English are already in Stirling. He thinks the battle is nigh. They are south of the bridge and the Scots are said to be on the other side hiding in the forest."

"Oh, my." Worry throbbed in her mind as she thought over and over again about her lads, Gabriel, Grainger, the Scots, the English, her parents, her sister.

Who would win? Probably the English.

It was usually the English.

"He shall return soon. He said he'd be back after dawn with a fresh loaf of bread."

She huddled back into the plaids to await his arrival, listening to the growls of hunger in her belly. She'd lost weight for sure. There had been plenty to eat in Edinburgh, but she'd been too worried about her lads to take advantage of it. The pain from her wounds had improved, since it had now been several days, but worry was her constant companion.

The sound of a horse carried inside, so she tiptoed to the entrance, peeking out with Wyot and praying it was Gabriel. Fortunately, it was, but she didn't like how quickly he moved.

"The English are at Stirling. Thousands of them, they say. Many travel on horseback but others are walking. They are already conferring with Wallace, asking for him to give up all he's fought for, to concede victory to King Edward's men. I intend to see what transpires. I would suggest that you stay here, but I doubt you'll agree to it, and I'd prefer not to leave you. You need protection, lass."

"Do ye intend to join the baron?" she asked, clutching the plaid around her tight.

"Nay. I would never back that fool, but I wish to know what takes place. 'Tis a major event transpiring near us." He stared at her, then moved over to wrap his arms around her. "You're shivering."

"It's getting colder."

"I know. It's the tenth of September. What is your choice, go or stay?"

"I wish to go but I don't think I can stay on the English side. Gabriel, I'm a Scot. Can you not understand how I feel?"

"Aye, I do. You need not get involved, but I'd like to see what happens. Who will dominate? It's an important battle for both sides." He tucked her head under his chin, opening his mantle to give her his heat. "But I'll not make you go. You decide. I will tell you that we are north of Stirling. When we reach it, we'll come in on the side where the Scots are hidden. I cannot promise what will happen then."

"Wyot?" she asked. "What will ye do?"

"I'll be going to watch the battle," the lad said, practically bursting with excitement. He ran out of the cave then, leaving them alone.

"I could leave you here, but I'll worry," Gabriel said, touching her cheek gently. "If I take you, I'll worry. I can't make the decision for you. You must decide. I'll be leaving in half the hour."

She stepped out of his warm embrace and reached for her hairbrush. "Then I suppose I'd better get ready."

An hour later, they left on three horses, though she had no idea how long it would take to get to Stirling. Their path to Abbey Craig took them past the inn they'd stopped at the other day. A few other riders were headed in the same direction.

"What do they know?" Cara asked.

"I've a mind to find out," Gabriel said, his brow furrowed. "Wait here with Wyot. I'm going to pay a quick visit to the inn to see if they've learned anything new. I'd rather not bring attention to you, so it would be best if you waited here."

She agreed with him, and Wyot led her to a secluded patch of trees as Gabriel rode off. He hadn't been gone long when a rider cut in front of them from the cover of the woods.

It happened so suddenly she didn't have time to react, but Wyot drew his horse in front of her, calling out to the rider. "I know ye from the inn. She sent ye away before. Leave her be."

It was Grainger. How had he found her? And why was he being so persistent? Grainger came alongside her horse, and although she attempted to hold onto her mount as tightly as she could, he managed to grab her off. He plopped her in front of him with a growl of pleasure. "Finally. Ye would no' agree to come peaceably, so now we do it my way."

"Leave her be," Wyot said fiercely, charging toward them.

Grainger tugged on the reins of his horse, taking her off into the trees away from the common path.

"Grainger, leave me be," she shouted. "Ye're hurting me. What are ye doing?" She fought and scratched, hoping to slow their travel until Gabriel would come after her. Her back screamed in pain, but she had to ignore it. Gabriel would come, wouldn't he?

"I tried to be nice, but ye did no' wish to be agreeable. I'll tell ye what I'm doing. I'm not inter-ested in marrying ye anymore. I'm taking ye to Baron Hepple. He has a reward out for ye and yer friend. I may no' be able to handle him, but I can handle ye until I get my coin. The English say they'll convince the Scots to surrender and there'll be no battle. If I'm on the right side, I'll get land I deserve after they surrender. And I'll have more coin from turning ye over to Hepple."

A gasp escaped Cara's lips. It shocked her that her countryman would surrender his loyalty so easily—and for coin, not to protect a loved one. She shook her head, fighting him, while Wyot rode back to the inn and shouted for Gabriel to return. She would not go back to the baron.

She had to fight—for herself and her lads.

Frantic to escape, she swung around and tried to scratch his face as they barreled across the coun-tryside. If she did not get away, she might never see her sons again.

Grainger punched her, delivering a wallop that

nearly toppled her off his horse, but he managed to grab her by the hair to keep her there. She screamed and looked over his shoulder, wincing from the pain.

Gabriel was nearly behind them, his bow notched and ready to fire.

Hellfire, he'd known that bastard was going to be nothing but trouble, but when he saw the man punch Cara, he became consumed with rage and the need for vengeance. He fired off five arrows before finally hitting his target in the flank, sending the horse into a shimmy of fear. Grainger fell off the beast, landing on one side, while Cara fell off the opposite side.

Gabriel jumped down and went after the man, tossing his bow aside and drawing his sword. Grainger stood up, now acting totally deranged. He pulled out a knife and charged directly at Gabriel, staggering a bit from his wounded side. It was as if he didn't notice Gabriel's giant sword. He only veered away at the last second, running away from him before he whirled around.

"Come at me, I dare ye to try," Grainger bellowed. "I'll kill ye and get my reward for yer head, too. Hepple declared ye a spy. He said anyone who brings ye and the lady in will be handsomely rewarded. He wants the lady alive but does no' care about ye."

Gabriel saw the shock on Cara's face, but he kept his focus on his opponent. "Cara, stand back!"

He was too late. Grainger grabbed her by the hair and jerked her to her feet, placing his dagger at her neck. "Stay back or I'll kill her. Drop yer weapon and the lad will tie yer hands. Do it or I'll slice her throat." The daft look in his eyes told Gabriel that he meant what he said.

Gabriel's stomach clenched as he saw the fear in her eyes. He hadn't been there for Della, but he would keep Cara from the same fate. He gave Wyot a sign they'd developed long ago, coughing loudly before dropping his weapon to the ground and holding both hands into the air.

"Go tie him," Grainger said, motioning to Wyot. "There's rope on my horse."

The lad's eyes went wide with fear as he grabbed the rope and stepped up to do the man's bidding.

Gabriel wished to shout with joy when the lad slipped a small dagger into his hand before loosely tying them together. The lad walked off and launched his next role in their gambit—tripping and falling with a loud scream off to the side of the villain.

Grainger turned his head and his body, giving Gabriel just the opening he needed. "Duck, Cara!"

She dropped to her knees, and he fired the dagger into the man's neck, embedding it deep in the side, bright red blood pulsing out of the wound as Grainger fell to the ground.

He retrieved his weapon, checked on Wyot and Cara, then searched the area for any other Scots or Englishmen hoping to gain a reward for their capture, but there was no one around. He sheathed his sword, found his bow, and handed it to Wyot. When he turned to Cara, he saw she was still frozen in shock.

He stopped a little in front of her, not wishing to scare her. "Cara, 'tis all right. He'll not bother ye again." He was glad the truth was finally out so he could speak freely in his true brogue.

Wyot wore his usual grin as he glanced from one to the other. "Wyot, put the bow on my horse.

"Aye, my lord."

She continued to stare, but then whispered, "Ye are truly a spy for the Scots?"

Gabriel smiled and stepped closer to her. "Aye, I'm a proud Scot, and I'll never side with Edward. He isnae my king. Is he, Wyot?"

Wyot nodded and crossed his arms emphatically. "We are both proud Scots. I've been with my lord for nigh a year."

"But…but…but…"

"Aye, I know ye are taking in too much," he said, lowering his voice as he moved close enough to cup her cheek. "I am a Scot like ye are. I'm sorry I was forced to deceive ye, but I have two goals besides the new one I gained when I came upon ye and yer lads. My main goal was to spy for Wallace and the Bruce. I couldnae put ye at risk."

"But where are ye from? The truth, if you please."

"'Tis a fair question and one I'll answer honestly." He dropped his hand, understanding that she needed to make sense of all the new information he'd just given her before he should try to reach out to her again. "I lived in the Borderlands and was out hunting when King Edward and the English came to overtake our town. I lost my wife in the battle, and I vowed revenge against the man responsible."

"Who?"

He answered her with only one word. "Hepple."

"Then why have ye no' killed him already? I dinnae understand how ye could stand by him." The look in her eyes nearly destroyed him.

"Aye, and 'tis verra nearly killed me. But personal vengeance was not my only goal. I pledged myself to Wallace and the Bruce after King Edward massacred our brethren in the Borderlands. Imagine how I felt when I came upon Baron Hepple and fifty knights ready to attack the Scots. So I changed my brogue, something that was easy for me, and pledged my loyalty to King Edward. I vowed to get all the information I could to Wallace before taking my revenge on Hepple, but then ye came along. I couldn't allow him to treat ye so. I feared if I was honest with ye, that ye might give us away in Edinburgh, so I played the part.

"The English are here. They stand on the far side of the river at Stirling Bridge. Did Grainger say anything else to ye about their plan?"

She still looked stunned as she slowly shook her head. Then her eyes widened and she said, "Aye. He said the English were certain the Scots were about to surrender."

"Then we must move quickly. We'll go to Abbey Craig and stay behind the foremost line of battle. We must get our information to Wallace. I can only hope I'll have the opportunity to kill Hepple in battle, but I doubt he will have the courage to fight. He'll hang back."

"My lads?"

"Dinnae worry about them. They are with a Scottish woman. Ye dinnae want them here now."

The stiffness in her shoulders finally gave way and she threw her arms around his neck, whispering, "Many thanks for everything, but mostly, I'm glad ye are a Scot."

He inhaled her sweetness, his eyes closing to relish in her scent and her softness, but he knew they had to continue on. "Come, much as I would love to hold ye in my arms, we must get our information to William Wallace." He motioned for Wyot to bring their horses. As soon as they were all mounted, they galloped toward the abbey, moving as fast as their horses would carry them.

⚡

When they finally drew close to Stirling Bridge, she could see the English on the far side of the bridge, their cavalry a daunting picture. Gabriel wanted them to stay far enough away to not be seen, though she had to admit she was surprised to see no Scots on this side of the bridge with so many English on the far side of the bridge.

There were more than a few English. In fact, rows of English took over the far countryside, the river between the Scots and the English making it feel as though they were farther away than they probably were.

The oddest part was there were no Scots to be seen anywhere.

"Where are the Scots? Are we in the wrong place? Is this not the Scots' side of the bridge?" she asked when they stopped their horses a good distance from the river and the bridge, peering through the forest to see what transpired.

"This is the right side. I suspect most are in the forests hiding, although I see some of them gathering on the hilltop known as Abbey Craig, where the trees are thick," Gabriel said, pointing to an area she hadn't noticed. "Fighting could break out at any time. I want you in a safe place so we'll head to an area behind the Craig. We won't go near the bridge."

They led their mounts a distance beyond Abbey Craig, away from the English, eventually finding a group of small homes with a stable nearby. "You two wait here by the stable and I'll see what transpires. I wish to find Wallace and tell him what Grainger said." He left and found his way to a group of Scots not far from the river. They were alone but for a few horses meandering through the field. Cara felt relieved when he turned back, but then he headed toward the forests when two men approached him. Wyot whispered in awe, "'Tis William Wallace. See the tall one in the front heading toward Gabriel? 'Tis him, I think."

The man was quite tall, even more so than Gabriel, and he had dark hair. She could tell the discussion was heated and what they discussed was of the utmost importance. But what surprised her more was the appearance of two friars on the bridge.

If she were to guess, Gabriel and Wallace were as surprised as she and Wyot were, the others hiding in the stables also wondering what to make of it. The friars made their way to Wallace while a couple of other men emerged from the forest to stand by the great man's side.

"That's Robert the Bruce, I think," Wyot whispered with excitement, though the distance was too great for them to know for certain.

Cara had no idea what was taking place in front of them, but her heart sang for a different reason. The man she'd fallen in love with was a true Scot, who now stood by two of the most admired men in the land.

A while later, the friars returned to the bridge, and the Scots headed to the top of the craig while Gabriel made his way back to them, a distance behind the hill.

His strides were smooth and powerful, the look on his face unreadable because she was too far away and his beard hid everything. How proud she was of this man making his way back to her.

To her!

While they waited, more Scots arrived, many volunteering to fight though they stayed hidden, women arriving to help where they could. Word had traveled quickly among the Scots and it made her fiercely proud. They were far enough away to be invisible to the bridge because the landscape was so unusual. Other Scots came from behind Abbey

Craig. She overheard them speaking of the plan to hide behind the craig to await Wallace's signal.

Another woman came to her and said, "Come. We are hiding in the cottages. Our manor is large enough for you to join us. We'll cook what we can. If they battle, we'll need to do some stitching, I'm sure."

Gabriel nodded and said, "Probably safest for you to stay with the women. The manor is the largest. I'll come for you when I can. The atmosphere could be changing soon. I'll follow you to see exactly where you'll be."

They hurried off in a group but Gabriel refused to share anything else. Once they were alone again, she asked, "What does all this mean? The friars? I dinnae understand."

He said, "The information you got from Grainger was extremely helpful. Since Wallace knows the English expect them to surrender, he invited them over through the friars. He'll wait until enough come across the bridge that they can battle, and then the Scots will attack. The English will only be able to cross the bridge two at a time, so the Scots can control what happens. Wallace and his men also sabotaged the bridge. If enough horses come across, it will collapse and chaos will reign. 'Tis what he's hoping for to help the Scots control the battle. Once that happens, the Scots will attack, and I foresee many deaths that you'll not wish to witness. 'Tis best if you are far away from the action."

He stepped closer and cupped her cheek before

he reached into his pocket and said, "Here. 'Tis my lucky charm. Something tells me ye should carry it during the battle." He handed it to her, a stone his sire had given him long ago.

She took the charm and ran her fingers across the small surface. "Ye think 'twill protect me?"

"Aye." He held his hand out to her and said, "Come, lass. Trust me. The English are already coming across the bridge, two at a time. Wyot, you will protect her."

"Can I no' help the Scots? I wish to do what I can," he begged.

"Aye, ye may help toward the back. But ye will also check on Cara every hour. Am I understood?"

"Aye, my lord," he said, his excitement at the impending battle something only the young would feel if she were to guess.

Afraid she'd not see him again, she reached for his hand and he clasped it. "Lass, I promise to protect ye, and when this is done, ye'll get yer lads back. In the meantime, promise me ye'll not take any chances."

She squared her shoulders and moved over to her horse, finding a log to stand on, but he came over to grab her waist. Although he'd intended to lift her, she fell against him, wrapping her arms around him and finally crying.

"Now ye cry? I thought ye'd be happy I'm a Scot."

"I am. I'm ecstatic that the man I'm falling in love with is a Scot, not an Englishman. I dinnae know how that would work out."

Gabriel hugged her back and kissed her until Wyot came up behind them. "Hurry, my lord," he said, his tone urgent. "I hear more horses' hooves."

"Come, the English cavalry are coming across. I will get you to a safe place and join my Scottish brothers in this fight."

He led them back far away from the forest to the manor reserved for the women and the wounded. After he left, she turned to Wyot and whispered, "Godspeed to the Scots."

⚭

For several hours, Cara bit her nails, waiting for the battle to end. Once a sizable number of the cavalry of Englishmen cleared the bridge, the Scots came out of the forests and down from the craig, brandishing spears and shouting their war cries for all to hear. The sound of a horn screeched across the landscape just before the bridge collapsed, sending many of the English into the water. Wallace himself went after the leader of the English forces, or so Cara heard. The Scots routed the English easily, many of them trying to get away by swimming back across the river.

She wasn't the only woman about, and she mostly spent her time in the manor, helping where she could. Several of them would sneak away and peek to see what transpired across Abbey Craig and the bridge, then return to update the others. She and about twenty other women cooked, cleaned, and helped the injured and the sick when they could. Keeping busy was a balm. When there was nothing to do, the waiting was nearly intolerable.

There were several piles of wool, so she began to work the wool into a scarf, something that would keep her busy. They were there for so long that she managed to finish a smaller scarf for Brice.

By the end, the English did indeed retreat, but they lost thousands in the interim while the Scots had only lost hundreds. The bridge was destroyed and the English who lived, many of them having swum back across the river, left the area completely, leaving dead bodies everywhere.

All Cara could think was the Scots had won a major victory at last. She would finally be reunited with her lads. How she prayed this would be the end of King Edward torturing her people.

She spent hours assisting the wounded Scots and making pots of vegetable stew for the men.

But her mind was on her sons. She wanted to go to them.

Where was Gabriel, and when would he take her away from this battlefield?

CHAPTER TWELVE

Xo

THE NEXT MORNING, GABRIEL FINALLY made his way back, bloodied and dirty but unhurt. She threw her arms around his neck and kissed him. "You are hale?"

"Aye, I am in one piece." He wiped his brow and clasped her hand, leading her away from the manor. "Come, we must talk. I have something I must see to." She followed him outside, to a quiet spot in the trees. He kissed the back of her hand and said, "I have something I must do. Ye'll be safe here. I promise to come back to ye as soon as I'm able."

Confused, she said, "But what must ye do? I dinnae wish to be parted from ye any longer."

"I'll leave Wyot with ye. Also remember that ye have my lucky stone. My father swore that if it was rubbed just so, he'd sense the need for help." He shrugged. "At the time, I thought he sounded daft, but he believed in its power. Said it would work for me if ever I needed it."

She said, "Take me with ye. I can help ye." Frantic that he was choosing to leave her, she gripped his hand tight. "But my lads. Ye could take me to them first. What if ye dinnae come back? I know not where they are."

"I dinnae have time to take ye there now, but I promise to return. I must do something that cannae wait."

He kissed her cheek and headed to his horse, whose reins were tied to a nearby tree.

She couldn't let him go. "Gabriel, please dinnae leave me."

"Forgive me, but I must."

The look in his eyes frightened her—and it also told her what he had planned. He was going for the man who had killed his wife. He patted his horse, freeing the reins.

She ran after him, crying out, "Where are ye going? 'Tis done. The Scots defeated the English. Ye've told me ye're a true Scot at heart. What draws ye away?"

He spun around and stared at her. "Vengeance. I cannae rest until I exact vengeance on the bastard who killed my dear Della. Can ye no' see I must do it for her?"

She'd known what he was planning, of course. His mission had driven him for months, years. "The baron? Is that who ye're chasing? Where will ye find him? I can help ye if ye must arrest him."

"Arrest him?" he said, his tone dark, mounting his horse. "Oh, I'll no' arrest him. I plan to torture him, just as he did to Della. Just as he did to ye. I love ye both. I owe ye both. I must go after him." The fury in his gaze told her he was not going to let this go easily. "I've searched the dead bodies. He's not there. The spineless bastard lives."

Cara had to convince him to leave his anger behind him. If he did as he wished, it would eat at him for the rest of his life. He would surely regret sinking to the villain's level. The thirst for vengeance had destroyed her husband—his cause had been just, but the darkness had festered in his soul until it rotted his insides. She couldn't bear to watch another fall into its talons. Especially not the man she loved.

"Gabriel, please," she begged. "Don't go after him."

She followed his horse, calling to him, but he ignored her this time. Finally, he turned back toward her. "I know ye think I'm daft, but why should I no' go after Baron Hepple? He killed my wife and tortured ye. Now he'll pay, just like the other English paid with their lives. I'll return for ye when 'tis finally done and no' before. He's the reason I spied for the Scots, so I could always know where to find him. So I could find my opportunity to get close to him. I'm just sorry I wasnae there to stop your lashing. Standing beside that bastard was the most difficult thing I've ever done. Hate is no' a strong enough word for him, and he will pay for his sins."

He shook the reins and set his horse into a fast gallop.

But she couldn't let him do it.

She chased down another saddled horse and jumped up onto its back, barely managing the feat, and followed the dust that rose up behind Gabriel's mount.

They chased through ravines and glens, through forests and open meadows. Many times, she feared she had lost him, but then he stopped abruptly.

Ahead was a small group of Englishmen. She held back in the trees for fear of what would happen because he was outnumbered three to one. What could she do to help him? Gabriel said something to two of the men, and to her surprise, they mounted quickly and disappeared. That left him face to face with the third man, and when she drew closer, she knew exactly who it was.

Thorley Tremaine, the Baron of Hepple, guffawed as he listened to Gabriel's words, though she was unable to make out their conversation. Then he stopped laughing and a shocked expression overtook his features, but it disappeared as soon as Gabriel hit him with his fist, two punches to his face and one to his belly, knocking him to the ground.

Hepple must have just discovered where Gabriel's true loyalties lay.

Gabriel grabbed a rope from his horse, then grabbed Hepple, dragging him toward a nearby tree. The man held his arm in an odd way as if he'd been injured in battle.

Would he really hang him? Commit murder in cold blood? To kill a man in battle was one thing, this would be another entirely.

Cara screamed his name and he stopped.

"Gabriel, please dinnae do this. If ye're caught, ye

could be arrested and hanged. I need ye. We need ye. I wish to get my lads and join ye in the Highlands. Please leave him be and come with me," she pleaded, hoping he would listen to reason, though at the moment she was not sure he was capable of it. He had the same look of determination George had possessed as he forced her to train, again and again, for a fight he had known all along they would lose.

"Nay, I willnae," he shouted. "He deserves this. Do ye no' know what he did? Did I no' tell ye how he killed my sweet Della?"

"Oh, Gabriel. Please. Forget him. He is no' worth yer effort. Ye cannae think doing the same to him will make it right." She stopped, wringing her hands in front of her as the man she loved paced furiously in front of her, swinging the rope as he walked.

"Allow me to tell ye exactly what happened, Cara. Mayhap ye'll understand if ye hear what he did. Did ye no' hear of how King Edward came into Berwick, wanted to take the Borderlands in England's name? How he took over the castle, then had his men go through the town and kill everyone, men, women, children? They killed thousands, so many that the river ran red from all the blood. And he wouldn't stop. Not until he walked through the city two days later, wanting to see the outcome of his orders. He saw something so despicable that he couldn't bear to let it continue. Even the man known as the Hammer of the Scots couldn't tolerate what he saw."

Gabriel hung his head and the sobs began to wrack his body, his hands going to his eyes to stop the tears.

"Gabriel, I'm so sorry." She stepped closer to him, hoping she could help him deal with this terrible memory.

He sobbed into her shoulder. "He made them stop when he saw his men killing a pregnant woman…"

"Nay…" she cried, her tears mixing with his, her hands covering her ears because she feared what would come next.

"Aye, my sweet Della. Baron Hepple and his men were caught murdering my dear Della. Such a despicable act that even the king put a stop to it. Although it happened too late for my wife."

Her heart wrenched at such a thought. "How did ye find out?"

"I saw her after they left. Della had started to deliver our bairn, so I brought her to the midwife. The midwife checked her, said she wasnae ready yet. That would no' be until the morrow or the following day because 'twas our first bairn." He paced back and forth in front of her as his mind agonized through the horrific details. "I thought the best way to protect her would be to battle the cruel English, to drive them back. I planned to return to her that eve, before she delivered our son. But 'twas too late." He tugged his hair so hard she feared it would tear from his head. Tears coursed down his cheeks.

If it were possible, listening to his tears caused

her to love him even more. His love for his wife, his passion for his beliefs, were so strong that it humbled her.

He stopped pacing and continued. "Even I would never guess he would commit such an act." His breath hitched as he stared at the ground. "I was wrong. When I returned and found her, I held her close and roared my rage, vowing vengeance on the bastard. Harold saw. He told me and helped me bury her body, and ever since, I've sworn vengeance on Hepple. He deserves to be flayed alive, tortured, beheaded, everything possible."

She sobbed and sobbed, but then his anger returned. "And I will see that he pays." He whipped around because the baron had started to groan from the blow he'd been dealt.

Cara reached his side and grabbed his upper arm. "Nay, please come with me. Leave him, Gabriel. If ye do as ye say, 'twill haunt ye for the rest of yer days."

He turned back around, shouting at her. "Can ye no' see? What he did haunts me every day that he lives. I must do it. 'Tis on my conscience to exact vengeance on him, for what he did to ye and to Della."

He left her then, returning to the baron, his look of determination unchanged.

"Gabriel, I beg ye. Come with me. We'll find my sons and live in the Highlands. I love ye, please dinnae do this."

Something flashed in his eyes, and suddenly he was once again the Gabriel she knew and loved.

He strode over to her, his face tear-stained yet determined. He gripped her hands and said, "Cara, if I do as ye ask, he'll live to kill more women and bairns. Can ye live with that? I cannae spend every night wondering who he'll torture next."

Her tears flooded her face, because she knew he was right. Where did the Lord stand on such an issue? Hepple was evil and needed to be stopped. Here in the middle of Scotland, there was no jury to pass judgment on him, no court, no sheriffs. The country was in a turmoil as long as infidels like Thorley Tremaine lived.

Gabriel's thumb came up to brush her tears away. "I prefer to spend my time loving ye every night, holding ye in my arms with no worry that he might follow us. He knows my heart now, my true loyalty. He set a reward for the capture of both of us. Shall I free him to follow us and torture us?"

Cara stared into the eyes of the man she loved, the man who had protected her sons without being asked, who had interrupted the bastard who'd attempted to destroy her with his lash and his words.

And it struck her that he was right. Freeing Hepple would help no one and might hurt many. The man might follow her or seek out her lads.

That was something she could not fathom. Her hand came up to Gabriel's chest and she whispered, "Do as ye see fit, but I cannae witness."

"I understand. I'm sorry, Cara, but I must do this."

Cara slowly turned around and walked away,

sobbing for the man she loved and the woman and son he'd lost. Then she stopped and said, "Gabriel?"

"Aye?" he asked, turning to her.

"Please do no' stoop as low as that vermin did. I understand you have to do what you must but be the stronger man that ye are. Make it quick. I wish for many years with ye, and I dinnae wish ye to be scarred with regret."

✗○

Cara mounted her horse and headed back to the manor near Stirling Bridge, following the fresh tracks she'd left in her haste. As she rode, she prayed for guidance from any guardian angels she had. She understood why Gabriel had made the decision to end Hepple's life, but she hated to think about it.

Her mother had always told her that guiding angels watched over her and would help guide her if she ever lost her way. She felt lost now.

Her mind shifted to her lads. It felt as if a thread had pulled taut in her chest, drawing her to them. She wanted to be with her sons. She needed them, and they needed her. When Gabriel returned, she'd ask him to take her to them immediately.

She reached the manor before dark, but the thought of leaving Gabriel alone bothered her. She located Wyot, who was busy assisting the injured on the battlefield. Her stomach revolted at all the blood so she stepped away, sucking in the fresh air and lingering on the periphery. Even so, she picked up on some talk she didn't like. Stories of families being driven from their homes in wake of the battle. English killing every Scot they saw. Scavengers roaming from home to home, randomly killing or stealing what they could.

After the last comment, she decided she could wait no longer. They may have won the battle, but their victory had inflamed the English. Which meant her boys were in more danger than ever. Looking for Wyot to let him know she was leaving, she couldn't find him. He'd been on the other side of Abbey Craig and now he'd disappeared. An odd feeling struck her. It was almost as if someone stood behind her and pushed her toward her horse.

Perhaps she did have a guardian angel.

She would have to find her sons on her own. Mounting her horse, she headed in the direction Gabriel had taken her before, the landmarks she'd memorized fresh in her mind.

Her lads were depending on her.

It didn't take her long to find the home. Although she made a few wrong turns, she didn't get lost for long. She'd taken careful note of the landmarks on the way, and her knowledge guided her now. Finally, she arrived near the house. Grateful for her strong sense of direction, she dismounted, thinking of the look on her sons' faces when they saw her again.

When she stepped up to the front of the home, she cursed herself for not having asked Gabriel more questions about their caretaker. At least he'd reassured her that the person was Scottish. She had no idea who she was looking for or who owned the home. But no one answered her knock. The only response that greeted her was an eerie silence she didn't like.

She opened the door, surprised to see it was unlocked. Though it used to be customary to leave doors unlocked, people had started exercising more care once the English had started attacking deep into Scotland. Or so she'd thought.

The place was deserted. Her heart leaped into her throat and she ran up the stairs, down into the kitchens in the back, all through the bedchambers.

Empty. They were all empty. Frantic, she checked the chambers again, searching for any evidence that her sons had been here—anything at all. She found nothing. Tears flooded her face and a hopelessness such as she'd never known overtook her senses.

She fell onto one of the beds in a smaller chamber, clutching a pillow, only to realize it carried Brice's smell, that sweet aroma only wee ones held, losing it sometime between five and ten years.

She inhaled again, holding the fabric close to her nose, knowing without a doubt that her son had slept here.

Where had they gone?

She rolled onto her side, hugging the pillow to her face, and sobbed until there were no more tears inside her. Reaching into her pocket, she pulled out Gabriel's stone and rubbed it, the only thing she could think to do.

CHAPTER THIRTEEN

✍

GABRIEL MOVED TOWARD THE PRONE body of the man he'd hated for so long, Thorley Tremaine, the Baron of Hepple. The man who'd ordered so many women and children to be killed. The man who was so despicable that even the king known as the Hammer of the Scots had stopped his massacre.

He deserved to die, to be tortured, to be hung up by his bollocks.

So why did the face of an angel haunt Gabriel, begging him to be the stronger man, to come with her to find her sons, to form a new life in the Highlands away from all the pain and tragedy in their country?

An odd sense of calm settled over him as he stared down at the cruel man who was so vulnerable at the moment. The little man who couldn't hurt Gabriel if he tried, not without a sea of knights behind him.

The kind of man who enjoyed brutalizing women because he was so weak.

Perhaps Cara was right. He found a rock nearby

and sat down, considering all they'd discussed as the sun lowered on the horizon. He had no idea how long he sat there, but some time later, he caught movement in the corner of his eye—the baron going for his weapon.

"You thought I was knocked out all this time, fool?" the man asked, grinning as he jumped to his feet. He charged toward Gabriel with his blade held high above his head.

It had all happened so quickly that Gabriel barely had enough time to react. But his instincts were faster that Hepple's, and he turned sideways and swung his sword at the man's chest, catching him across his ribs, halting his forward movement instantly.

Gabriel looked into Tremaine's eyes and said, "This is for my Della." When the bastard fell to the ground, his face slack with shock, Gabriel plunged his blade deep into his heart. Hepple gurgled and gave one last squeal before the life force drained out of his body.

Gabriel stepped back after retrieving and cleaning his weapon, a sigh of relief escaping his mouth involuntarily, as if the wound deep in his gut had finally left him, freeing him from the constriction it had held on him for so long. Rubbing his eyes, he realized he did gain a certain pleasure knowing the bastard would never torture another woman or child. Even more so because he had not disrespected himself, Della, or Cara.

He heard his name called from afar and turned around to see who'd said it. Immediately, he knew it to be Wyot, dear Wyot, who had helped him along on this sordid journey. But there was one difference.

Wyot wasn't smiling anymore. He searched again for the sun, wondering how long he'd been here.

"My lord, my lady was alone. I saw her at the battlefield where I was assisting the wounded, but then she disappeared. I headed to the manor where her sons were hidden because 'twas the only place I could think of that would draw her." He stopped for a moment to catch his breath. "They're not there. She's devastated. She was lying on a bed with a pillow near her face, staring into the ceiling. It was verra odd. She never knew I was there. What shall I do?"

"Shite," he said, casting another glance at the baron. "All right. I'm finally done here, lad."

"Ye killed him?" Wyot asked, wide-eyed.

"He came at me first, lad. I had no choice, but aye, I killed him." Surprised, he found that the scenario had unfolded just as it should. He'd spent many months imagining how he could torture Hepple when the cruel man was finally at his mercy. He'd killed him, and his need for vengeance was done. He strode over to the baron and kicked him again, needing at least that, then he grabbed the reins of the man's horse and led him over to Wyot. "We're taking his horse. The buzzards can have what's left of him."

"But my lady... We must hurry."

"I'll get her, dinnae worry." He stared up at the sky, his hands on his hips, wondering why the Lord had sent this wee lass and her boys to him, instilling in him such a desperate need to protect her that he could not follow through on his plans for the ultimate vengeance. The irony of that was not lost on him.

A sudden warmth in his heart caused him to reach for his stone, interrupting his thoughts. Then he remembered he'd given it to Cara. Was his sire right? Could she be calling him through his stone?

He couldn't help but chuckle at the outrageous thought, but it rang true, nonetheless. "Wyot, we have to go after her. I know. When we get closer, I'll send you to the inn for some food, bread, oat-cakes, anything you can bring us. We shall all need sustenance."

Wyot's smile had been restored. "Aye, my lord. Will ye marry, do ye think?"

"If she'll have me. But I'm such an arse, she may no' want me."

He mounted and they moved along without any interference from anyone. The English had lost many men, and the lack of activity on the paths was the most solid evidence of their defeat other than the number of bodies they'd seen.

When they neared the fork in the path, he waved Wyot off to the inn. He knew the scene inside the manor was not going to be a pleasant one. He stopped directly in front of the place, noting her horse hadn't deserted her, fortunately. He gave the beast a pat on its flank and a small apple.

The manor was deserted, just as he'd expected. He stepped inside the door quietly, listening for the sound of sobbing, but heard nothing. The sun would be dropping soon, so he found a torch and lit it. Though he could still see well enough, the light wouldn't last for long.

Wyot had mentioned a bedchamber, so he climbed the stairs and peeked inside each chamber until he found her.

It was worse than he'd have guessed. He set the torch in a holder in the passageway after lighting a tallow in the chamber. "Cara?"

Nothing. She lay on the bed like a stone statue, unmoving, still clutching a pillow against her chest. He sat on the bed and leaned over to kiss her cheek. "Cara, 'tis me. You were right. I couldn't do it in the end. Ye are more important to me."

Still nothing. Her eyes were open but unfocused. He passed his hand in front of her face, but her eyes didn't move. It was as if she didn't see anything.

"Sweetling, I moved the boys."

Thankfully, her head turned to gaze at him. She whispered, "My lads are gone. I have no one." He expected to see a tear, but there was nothing.

"Aw, lassie." He picked her up as gently as he could and cradled her like a wee bairn, sitting on a chair. "Nay, ye have me. And yer sons are fine. I moved them to another place when I learned the battle could bring the English near here."

"Ye did? Ye moved them? Do they live?" The hope in her gaze was like a fist to his gut because he'd done this to her by not telling her. He feared she'd be kidnapped and forced to reveal their location, and he had a stake in this, too.

"Aye, they live, and I'll take ye there on the morrow, but ye must answer one question for me."

She sighed, her fingers touching his lower lip, her gaze searching his face. "I'm so glad ye've returned to me." She leaned forward and kissed him, drinking from him as though she'd been desperate for days, a mewling sound coming from the back of her throat that nearly unmanned him. Needing to ask his question of her, he ended the kiss.

"My question? Please? Ye are distracting me."

"What?" she whispered.

"I love ye. Will ye marry me, Cara Breckenridge?"

Her eyes lit up. "Aye, I *will* marry ye. Ye've pleased me and protected me so much."

"But do ye love me? Do ye still have feelings for me after I let ye walk away? I regret that I was in a fury I could no' control. I dinnae want yer pity, lass, I need yer love." He didn't know how to explain to her that her answer meant everything to him, that he believed her love and support would empower him to do and survive anything. There would be more tough times ahead.

"Aye, I love ye with all my heart, Gabriel Montgomerie, and I loved ye even when I thought ye were English." She smiled and he chuckled, kissing her again.

This time, she ended the sweet kiss. "Make love to me, please? Now? I wish to be as one with ye."

He growled, picked her up and set her down next to the bed before dropping his clothes and helping her remove her own. "Do ye know how long I've dreamt of this, lass?"

His need for her took over. "Cara, ye are so beautiful." He placed a trail of kisses down her neck, across her fine bone, down to her breast, his teeth grazing across her nipple and bringing it to a taut, rosy peak.

She arched against him, her fingers threading through his hair and gripping him tight as he continued the tantalizing assault on her breasts, moving from one to the other and back again. His need for her consumed him, and he did what he could to bring out the passion he suspected she carried deep inside her. He lifted her into his arms, their gazes locking as he set her under the covers, the tallow he'd lit casting a golden shadow over her skin.

"Ah, sweet Cara. Ye know no' how it pleases me to know ye are mine," he whispered against her neck, arranging the covers over them to keep them warm in the cold manor. She shivered beneath him, so he hastened to cover her body with his own. "Shall I start a fire?"

She shook her head, a saucy grin crossing her lips. "Nay, ye are the only heat I need. If we can survive in a cave, I'm sure we'll be fine here."

He kissed her, his tongue tasting and teasing her, but he found he couldn't wait much longer. "Take me, sweetling. Take me inside ye, show me ye love me."

She spread her legs to ease his entrance and reached for him, the heat of her hand nearly sending him into an early finish, but he vowed to control himself. The way she teased him across her slick folds was akin to torture, but after a few minutes, she opened for him and settled him where she wanted him.

"Fill me, Gabriel. I want all of ye."

Cara had a sudden understanding of life that she'd never known was possible. Lying in the arms of this man she loved, giving herself to him, and seeing the pleasure they gave each other was the most wonderful experience she'd ever shared with anyone. As their bodies melded together as one, she wrapped her hands around his neck and gazed up at him. She gave a small sob of pleasure, that feeling of fullness swaying her insides with a pleasure wholly new to her.

There was no pain, no hurry, no rush to finish. Instead he stared back at her, filling her completely until he began a slow rocking inside her, building a need that only he could.

She joined him in his rhythm, increasing the pace when she needed to, still holding his gaze. After a time, he closed his eyes and whispered, "Cara, my sweet Cara. Have we no' known each other forever?"

He pulsed against her, driving her need to the edge of a precipice she'd never known before. His thrust drove into her again and again, and she held her breath, waiting for whatever else he would give her until she exploded over the edge, calling out his name, her nails digging into his shoulder.

He plundered her until he stiffened with a loud groan that turned into a dull roar, the throbbing deep inside her continuing to give her pleasure as he finished.

He nuzzled against her, whispering her name, "Cara mine. I love ye."

His words brought tears to her eyes, tears of happiness at the beauty of what they had found together. He tried to pull out but she stopped him. "No' yet. I like ye where ye are."

He chuckled and nibbled her neck. "As do I." He held his weight up on his elbows and said, "We're finding the first kirk we can so I can pledge myself to ye. Agreed?"

"Agreed."

She'd never been so happy. The only thing that could make it better was to be reunited with her lads.

One step at a time.

The next day, the sun was at its highest point when Wyot called out to them. "'Tis around the next bend. I know it."

She glanced up at the deep cloud cover, searching out the sun's muted glow. Gloomy or not, she would marry this man today, and she hoped for a life of happiness with him. Sure enough, they came upon a small but beautiful kirk along the most traveled path to the Highlands. Wyot jumped off his horse and said, "I'll go."

"Lad," Gabriel barked. "Please stay with Cara.

There are Englishmen hiding around the country-side. I see a lone horse behind the kirk, and I need to see who it belongs to before we move forward. I'll check."

"Aye, my lord." His expression turned serious, just as it always did when he was given an order. The lad took his responsibilities very seriously.

Just as Bryan did. Soon she'd see her sons again, a thought that made her heart glow brighter than the sun. She looked forward to introducing them to Wyot. Something told her they'd get along.

As Gabriel approached the kirk, a large figure stepped out of the front door, followed by a smaller robed figure. "We've been waiting for you," Harold said, giving them a broad smile and a wink."

"How did ye know we'd be here?" Gabriel asked.

"I know more than you think. I'm not just a cook. Come inside." He introduced the priest behind him as Father Mac Neil.

They were married on that quiet day in the Highlands, Wyot standing next to her and Harold standing next to Gabriel. And it was perfect in all ways but one: her sons were not there.

So happy to be marrying this man, Cara hardly heard any words the priest said, instead thanking God for bringing Gabriel to her when she was so desperately in need, and for helping the Scots to stand tall against the English.

"Please kiss your bride," said Father Mac Neil.

She sighed as Gabriel's lips settled on hers, a gentle warm assault coupled with giggling and

applause from Wyot and a loud whoop from Harold.

They were husband and wife.

CHAPTER FOURTEEN

THE GROUP OF FOUR ARRIVED at a manor in the Highlands two nights later. Since they'd met up with Harold for the wedding, he'd been pleased to join them as they moved away from the common battleground.

Gabriel helped her down and she said, "'Tis much colder here. I hope the lads are hale."

"Your lads are strong. Ye need no' worry so," he said, grabbing the saddlebags and handing one off to Wyot.

But she couldn't move her feet. "Wait, please. Gabriel, ye never told me who watches them."

"My mother watches them. My father passed away long ago from a fever, but she has loved them like her own grandbairns, sweetling."

Warmth washed over her, but her feet still wouldn't move. He headed toward the front door, just then noticing that she wasn't moving. "Cara? 'Tis no reason for ye to fear this," he said, stopping to turn around to face her. "Why the hesitation? Ye've waited for this."

"What if…" How could she explain her fears to

him? "What if they hate me for leaving?"

She didn't have to worry much longer. The door opened and her two boys burst out of the house, racing toward her. "Mama?" Brice called out. "'Tis it ye, truly? I've missed ye so much."

She held her arms open and Brice launched himself at her first, and to her surprise, Bryan hugged her tightly, too.

"We missed ye so much, Mama," Bryan said. "Are ye here to stay or can we no' go with ye now?"

Tears burst from her eyes, drenching her cheeks in seconds as she hugged the boys and said prayers of thanks for this moment. "Please," she whispered. "Allow me to look at my fine lads. Please?"

She cried so hard she didn't think she'd ever stop.

"Why do ye cry?" Brice asked, staring up at her. "Are ye leaving us again?"

She laughed and squeezed him again. "Nay, never. These are happy tears, laddie."

Brice giggled and hugged her again.

It was then that she realized she'd ignored Gabriel. "Lads, I'd like ye to meet my new husband. This is Gabriel Montgomerie, and we will live with him, though I know not where exactly."

"But he's English, Mama," Bryan said, his expression turning to stone. "I remember him."

Gabriel stepped up to the boy who nearly reached his shoulders. "Nay, I am a true Scot. I spied on the English to help Robert the Bruce and William Wallace. And Wyot and I—" He brought his friend forward. "—we both watched over yer mother. I love her, and I'm sorry ye lost yer father.

I hope ye'll accept me in yer home. I'm asking for yer acceptance. After all, ye are now the eldest male in yer family."

"But where will we live?" Brice asked.

"If ye all agree, we can live here," he said, glancing over his shoulder as the door opened again and an older woman stepped out. She made her way over to them, wrapping a shawl tightly over her shoulders, her gray hair neatly plaited and pinned up. Gabriel kissed her cheek, then introduced her. "This is my mother, Hestra."

Cara couldn't have been more surprised. "This place belongs to ye, Gabriel?" While it wasn't large, it was well built, a stone cottage with a thatched roof over a building that had to hold at least four chambers. It even had a second story, something rarely seen.

"It does, and because of its location, I believe we'll be safer from the English here in the Highlands. They rarely come this far north. I have a small castle in the Lowlands, but I think this would be better. What say ye? And Harold here is the best cook ever, lads. He'll make the best meat pies ye've ever tasted. There are plenty of beds for all of us here."

He took her hand and led the group inside the front door. Cara stepped into the main chamber, turning around to admire the impressive size, the warm hearth at the back, and all the special touches his mother had added—cushions, dried flowers, warm plaids hanging over every chair. "'Tis lovely."

Hestra came up behind her. "I'm pleased ye like

it, and I must say, I've grown fond of yer laddies. They are fine boys. I hope ye'll stay."

Brice smiled and cheered, jumping up and down. "Here, I want to stay here."

Bryan looked from one to the other and said, "I'd prefer to stay here, where 'tis safe. I dinnae wish to see the English again." He looked up at his mother thoughtfully, then looked back to Gabriel. "And I'm pleased ye've married my mother, that is, if he's kind to ye, Mama."

Taken aback that he would ask that, she realized her eldest had been more aware of her situation in the past than she'd given him credit for. "He is, Bryan. Gabriel is a kind and thoughtful man."

Gabriel clasped Bryan's shoulder and said, "We willnae forget yer father." Then he released him and turned toward Cara. "I only have one person yet to hear from." He tipped his head, awaiting her answer.

She gave him a quick kiss on the lips and said, "This is perfect."

EPILOGUE

GRAEME (GABRIEL) AND CATHERINE (CARA) stood on the peak of a large hill in the Highlands, his arms wrapped around her as they watched the shenanigans taking place in front of them. Their children and their grandchildren sat on various homemade sleds and sped down the incline, their laughter lighting up their day.

Tessa appeared next to them, wrapped in a heavy wool mantle. "I think I preferred the beach," she said, shivering. "I don't have many clients who wish to return to the cold."

Catherine said, "Our apologies, but we miss watching our family. Their laughter is a boon to our souls."

Tessa sighed as her gaze fell on the youngest, about two years old probably, who tried to stand up in the deep snow but kept falling back onto his bottom. "Understood. You have a lovely family. Four boys and three girls, and how many grandchildren?"

"Twelve at present. Aren't they beautiful?"

"They are," Tessa said. "And I love that you found

your mother and your sister not far from your home."

Catherine gave her an odd look. "Did you have anything to do with that? I was sad to find my father had passed, but I so enjoyed living near my sister."

Tessa winked. "I may have had a hand in it. Come with me to chat for a bit?"

Graeme said, "Of course." He kissed Catherine's forehead and said, "We can come back afterward."

Tessa waved her hand and the scene around them changed. Suddenly, they were in a small cottage overlooking a lake, sitting on a porch where they could hear the lapping of the water against the shore. "This is my little slice of heaven. I love the lakes. So tell me about your experiences. What was easy? What was difficult?"

Graeme looked at Catherine and said, "You go first."

She thought for a moment, then said, "Not knowing where my boys were was one of the worst forms of torture. I couldn't relax until I started to trust Gabriel."

"And what made you trust him?" Tessa asked.

"I'm not sure when it started, but I felt pretty sure of him by the time he came for me after the baron gave me the lashes."

"But your trust was put to the test when the boys weren't waiting for you in the manor. I was worried we'd put you through too much," Tessa said. "You both were sorely tested on this journey. What kept you from giving up? It's always a question we have of human nature."

Catherine turned to Graeme and said, "He brought me back. The sound of his voice, the warmth in his being...it healed me. Rubbing the stone he'd given me calmed me in an odd way. When he came to me, I knew I could trust him forever."

"Your toughest part, Graeme?"

"I'm sure you know what I'll say, but facing the baron was the hardest challenge for me."

Tessa angled her head. "Did you enjoy killing the man?"

He considered that for a moment, brushing the dark shadow of his beard. "No, but I believed it was fair. Before Catherine came to me, I'd planned on torturing him, but something she said to me changed my mind. She told me to be the stronger man. That stayed with me."

"Did you tell her exactly what happened?"

"No, I never knew the full story," she said, holding his hand in hers. Looking into his eyes, she added, "But I knew anyway. I knew you could never torture anyone."

Tessa nodded as if pleased. "That man would have killed many more people had you let him live, Graeme, so you saved them by defending yourself. It's a difficult concept we still deal with here in Heaven. When is killing the best choice? Each case is individual."

"So we both passed our test?" Catherine asked, giving him a grin. "Do we continue in our quest to earn our wings?"

Tessa got up from the table and moved over to a spot where she could see the entire lake. "You both have done well. You will continue your quest with one more life, but first we'll give you a month to enjoy Heaven. You may travel wherever you like, but please come back to visit me once your time is up, though you may receive a different angel. Any plans for what you wish to do?"

They looked at each other and shrugged their shoulders in unison. Graeme said, "As long as we're together, I don't care where we go."

"Your next test could be your last."

"Do you know where we travel?"

"No, not yet. But it will definitely be the most difficult challenge you've ever faced."

THE END

A NOTE FROM KEIRA

As often happens when an author researches a specific time period, a little detail will catch us so much that we write an entire story around it. That happened to me when I read about King Edward and the massacre at Berwick. Part of me hates to include horrendous details, but if they are true, I find it haunting. I needed to say something about that pregnant woman who lost her life to a cruel massacre. While Hepple is fictitious, the situation was true.

The Battle of Stirling Bridge took place in 1297. This is not to be confused with the Siege of Stirling Castle, which took place in 1304 without the same success.

I tried to stay true to history in regards to the Battle of Stirling Bridge, but other than two small cameos from William Wallace and Robert the Bruce, my characters are all of my own creation. The story is true about the English coming across the bridge, two at a time, to accept the Scots' surrender, only to be ambushed. It was indeed William Wallace who fashioned something that caused the bridge to collapse as the English came across.

I view my storytelling as historical romantic suspense. It's not always roses, but they will always have a happy ending.

For those of you who were wondering, Wyot was Cara's guardian angel and Harold was Gabriel's.

Until the next time!

As always, reviews would be greatly appreciated. Sign up for my newsletter on my website at *www.keiramontclair.com*. I send newsletters out with each new release.

Another way to receive notices about my new releases is to follow me on BookBub. Click on the tab in the upper right-hand side of my profile page. You can also write a review on BookBub.

Keira Montclair

www.keiramontclair.com
www.facebook.com/KeiraMontclair
www.pinterest.com/KeiraMontclair

NOVELS BY

KEIRA MONTCLAIR

ABOUT THE AUTHOR

KEIRA MONTCLAIR IS THE PEN name of an author who lives in Florida with her husband. She loves to write fast-paced, emotional romance, especially with children as secondary characters.

When she's not writing, she loves to spend time with her grandchildren. She's worked as a high school math teacher, a registered nurse, and an office manager. She loves ballet, mathematics, puzzles, learning anything new, and creating new characters for her readers to fall in love with.

She writes historical romantic suspense. Her bestselling series is a family saga that follows two medieval Scottish clans through three generations and now numbers over thirty books.

Contact her through her website,
www.keiramontclair.com.